WINTER'S WAR

THE BLUE SIDED HUMAN WILL CHOOSE A SIDE.
WHEN FOUR PRINCES ARE BORN ON THE SAME DAY, THEY WILL RULE TRUE.
HER SAVIOUR WILL DIE WHEN THE CHOICE IS MADE.
IF SHE CHOOSES WRONG, SHE WILL FALL.
IF SHE CHOOSES RIGHT, THEN SHE WILL RULE.
ONLY HER MATES CAN STOP HER FROM THE DESTRUCTION OF ALL.
IF THE FATES ALLOW, NO ONE NEED FALL.
FOR ONLY THE TRUE KINGS HOLD HER FATE, AND THEY WILL BE HER MATES.

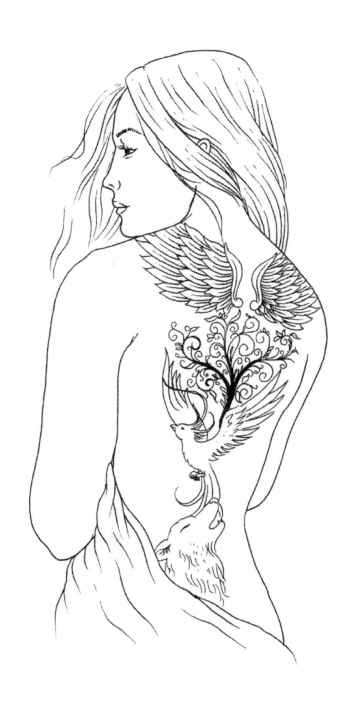

WINTER'S WAR

HER GUARDIANS SERIES BOOK FOUR

G. BAILEY

MORE BOOKS BY G. BAILEY

HER GUARDIANS SERIES

HER FATE SERIES

PROTECTED BY DRAGONS SERIES

LOST TIME ACADEMY SERIES

THE DEMON ACADEMY SERIES

DARK ANGEL ACADEMY SERIES

SHADOWBORN ACADEMY SERIES

DARK FAE PARANORMAL PRISON SERIES

SAVED BY PIRATES SERIES

THE MARKED SERIES

HOLLY OAK ACADEMY SERIES

THE ALPHA BROTHERS SERIES

A DEMON'S FALL SERIES

THE FAMILIAR EMPIRE SERIES

FROM THE STARS SERIES

THE FOREST PACK SERIES

THE SECRET GODS PRISON SERIES

THE REJECTED MATE SERIES

FALL MOUNTAIN SHIFTERS SERIES

ROYAL REAPERS ACADEMY SERIES

THE EVERLASTING CURSE SERIES

DESCRIPTION

The blue-sided human will choose a side.
When four princes are born on the same day, they will rule true.
Her saviour will die when the choice is made.
If she chooses wrong, she will fall.
If she chooses right, then she will rule.
Only her mates can stop her from the destruction of all.
If the fates allow, no one need fall.
For only the true kings hold her fate, and they will be her mates.

The prophecy is true, the war is here, and her saviour will die.
Reverse harem series

CHAPTER 1

ATTICUS

*W*ake her up, wake her up, new king. For the crown will fall, the crown will fall. The crown will fall . . . .

The shaking of the ground wakes me up from my deep sleep and the strange dream. I can't remember anything other than words about waking someone up and the child-like voice that sang them. I glance over at Winter, who is pressed to my side, her arms wrapped around a pillow. The room is still dark, the stars lighting up the sky outside, and it's cold. Colder than I remember it being when we fell asleep. Winter moves slightly, rolling onto her stomach, her soft, dark hair spreading across the pillow. *My mate.*

I smile when I see the marks on her back, a

beautiful reminder of last night. I've waited so long to be mated to her, to my Winter. We finally have everything, and even with her grandfather causing issues, I know we will make it through this. I didn't wait this long to mate with her only to lose her. That is never happening.

The room shakes again, and this time, I know it's not a dream that woke me up. I sit up and pull myself out of bed, careful not to wake Winter up. The room shakes again as I throw on some jeans and a shirt. *What the fuck is going on?*

I storm out of the bedroom, and there's a dark witch outside, her head covered by her cloak hood, so I can't speak into her mind. When she lowers her hood, I see that she is an older woman I don't know, but she bows to me. *Where are the guards?*

"Watch Winter, and do not let anyone in this room. If she wakes up, tell her to stay inside," I say, knowing full well Winter wouldn't stay inside, but I hope that she doesn't wake up. At least, this witch will be able to tell her where I am. The witch straightens up, and her dark grey eyes watch me closely before looking at the door behind me.

"Yes, your highness," she says in my mind. I pull on my power to lead me to the throne room and hope I can find some answers there, if nowhere else. The

room is in chaos when I appear in the middle of it. There are at least fifty demons in the room attacking my witches. One runs straight at me, with a large silver sword and an emotionless look in his eyes. The demons look worse than the last time I saw any of them; the grey skin is peeling off their faces in places, and the smell from them is over-whelming. They smell like death. I quickly pull on my fire power and throw a line of fire towards him with my hand. The demon-possessed man doesn't even move out of the way as the flames head towards him and burn him into nothing. There was no scream, and that's the weird part. It's like he didn't feel anything. *How can you fight against demons that don't care if you hurt them?* A loud growl gets my attention, and I look over to see my familiars, Mags and Jewels, jumping onto demons and using their large teeth to rip the heads right off them. I kill more demons as I make my way over to them.

"They want the queen," a witch runs over to me. I cover her from the two demons following her by using my wind power to throw them through the glass windows, smashing the windows to pieces. Witches with the air gift start to copy what I did and start throwing them through the windows rather than trying to kill them in here. I look over at the witch, who has a deep cut down her face and black ash covering her, mixed with blue dust from the dead demons.

"How do you know that?" I ask, lowering my hands a little but keeping an eye on the enemies around us. The castle shakes once more, followed by a loud howl that I recognise as Jaxson's. I forgot he was staying at the castle tonight. Everyone else went back to the goddess's castle.

"The demon king let Taliana's parents out from the dungeons. I was there, and the he said he wants Winter," the woman pleads. She looks familiar, but I don't know her. She clearly cares about Winter, and that's enough for me to believe her. I pull on my power to try and find her, it doesn't work. I can't feel her, only darkness. *No.*

I use my power to take me to my bedroom and find our bed empty, a feeling of dread fills my stomach. I pull the door open to find the older, dark witch is gone. The castle shakes again, and I use my power to find Jaxson. There isn't a witch strong enough to move the ground like this, and knowing Jaxson, he would be outside. The whole castle is shaking as I disappear, and I know it's lucky the castle doesn't fall. I appear in the gardens. What was once a beautiful place is a disaster. The trees are on fire, and a dead witch looks up at the sky from beside my feet. My mind goes to Winter when I look down at the dark witch's hair, which is only a little darker than my Winter's. I cannot lose her. I stand straighter when two demons run at me, their grey skin giving them away, as well as the empty look in their eyes. They have big, silver swords raised at their sides, and I use wind to divert the fire in the trees towards them. They don't stop running as they burn, the awful smell filling the night, but I bet they are better off dead than having a demon in their bodies. I lean down and close the witch's eyes. She is so young, and it's a shame her life ended like this. A growl gets my attention, and I look to my right, seeing Jaxson.

Jaxson has split a hole down the middle of the royal gardens that you can't miss, and it's smart, as my witches are pushing demons into the hole. Jaxson is in wolf form and is ripping the heads off demons as he runs past. He is massive like this, taller than a human and at the right level to kill them easily. His black fur is covered in blood and blue dust, and I know he must have been fighting since the start of the attack. Two witches run up to me, and I use my air power to push three demons following them into the hole.

"There are too many, Your Highness," one witch says, and she must only be sixteen by her looks.

"Go to the goddess's castle," I tell them both and send an image of the castle into their minds.

"Thank you," she says and disappears with her silent friend. I look over to see some are using wind, and most are using fire; I'm proud of how they are working together. I try to find Winter again, finding I can't. There's nothing, but I'm not giving up. *I will find her.*

"Jaxson!" I roar into his mind when a demon runs at him from behind with a large, silver sword aimed at his head. I pull my power and lift the demon off the ground, throwing him into the hole, but it gets Jaxson's attention as his glowing, green eyes lock onto mine across the fire and death that surrounds us.

"Winter is gone!"

Even over the witches' screams, the distance between us, and the noise from the shaking ground, Jaxson's threatening growl fills the night; a growl that speaks of pain, revenge, and a promise. We will find our queen.

CHAPTER 2

JAXSON

"*W*here is she?" I growl out when Atti gets to me through the demons he kills on the way. A demon runs at me, and I grab him by the neck, lift him up in the air, and watch as he dies. The clothes he was wearing fall to the ground, and I look down. I shake the blue dust off the jeans he was wearing and pull them on, thankful they fit at all. Atti stops walking toward me to throw a demon into the hole. I pick up a silver sword off the ground by the leather handle and quickly run, swinging it down on the head of a demon that leans over a dead witch. Atti lifts his hands, using air to throw two more demons into the hole, and then ducks when another witch does the same and throws a demon over his head. I woke up to this madness when five demons came into my room. They got a shock when I shifted and killed them all, or they would have if they didn't fight like emotionless zombies. It took me a long time to even get to the gardens, killing countless demons that I came across. I tried to help the witches in the gardens, but there were, and still are, so many demons here. So, I made a hole for them to throw the demons in. Otherwise, the ones without the fire power had no defence and no weapons. If there are this many in the castle, then the screams I can hear from the city tell me there are just as many out there. They are dying, and all I can think of is what Atti said, that Winter is gone. *He has to be wrong.*

"I can't find her, I can't sense her, Jax," he says, his words filling me with panic. She can't be dead, I would know. Our mate isn't dead. Yet I can't feel her like I would usually be able to. I can't sense her around, and Atti wouldn't just say this.

A demon runs at us, and Atti shoots a fireball at him, burning a hole in his chest, and the demon collapses into blue dust. I stomp over to a demon who is holding a young witch on the ground. She is struggling to hold him off with her air power.

"The whole city is under attack. Atti, you're their king. You need to tell them to go to the castle!"

I shout as I pull the demon off the witch on the ground, throwing him into the hole. Winter would never forgive us if we let our feelings cloud our minds over the responsibility we have to these witches. We can't just leave them. Atti closes his eyes, his body glowing a yellow colour as he tells the whole city to leave:

"Everyone leave and go to the goddess's castle. It's safe. I'm showing you the image now. Everyone go, leave the city, and you will be safe."

I hear the same thing that the witches do, and they start disappearing. Atti stumbles a little, his hands going to his knees as he takes a deep breath. *That must have been a fucking lot of power.* I grab Atti's arm, shaking him a little, and he nods at me. This isn't the time to give up. We need to find Winter, and we can't do that here. He straightens up and flashes us back to the goddess's castle, straight to Wyatt and Dabriel, who are pacing Winter's bedroom.

"Winter feels gone, where is she?" Wyatt shouts, walking over to us, and Dabriel follows. They both look as panicked as we feel. A feeling of sickness is spreading all over me, and I don't know what to do. I can't fucking do anything.

"I can't feel her," Dabriel says, and I nod,

feeling the same. I feel empty, the place inside me where she was is hollow now. *I can't sense her.*

Fucking hell, she'd best be alive, or I'm going to destroy the world until I find her or kill myself doing so. There isn't a life without Winter. I can't lose her, not now. The only person that could have taken her is her grandfather—the demon king. It wouldn't surprise me because I have a feeling he needs her for something.

"The demon king has her, doesn't he?" I ask, and there's silence from all of them.

"You remember that witch, the one that poisoned Winter and a demon killed her?" I ask them all.

Dabriel replies, "I remember. You think the demon king was protecting her?"

"Yes. He needs her for something, so that means he won't kill her. We would all know if she were dead."

"We have to find her. Whatever he wants her for is nothing good," Wyatt says and then mutters a string of curses to the room. We all feel the same way.

"Wait, I feel her," Atti says and grabs our arms.

I feel a flicker of something just before Atti takes us to Winter. To our mate.

"**W**inter," I breathe out when Atti' bring us near her, but there's a massive blue barrier between us. She is standing next to the huge crystal that keeps the witches' island protected from the world. There are dozens of little cracks in the crystal that shouldn't be there, and the shaking ground is making more sense now. He is trying to drop the ward on the city, but why? It makes no sense as his demons can clearly walk straight through wards. I guess it would make the witches vulnerable, but we were right, he has her.

The demon king is standing next to her, his hand on her shoulder. I don't look at him for more than a second as Winter ignores us. I've never seen her look like this, the way she looks at me. Her eyes are silver, completely silver, as she rests her hands on the crystal, and she is glowing blue, the way she does when she uses her power, but it's darker. The blue almost looks unnatural compared to the light colour it usually is. The way she looks at us all makes me wonder if she recognises us at all.

"Winter," Atti shouts, moving forward and banging his hands on the blue barrier which is stopping us getting to her. Atti's hands glow white as he tries to break the barrier, but it doesn't work. I can tell that nothing happens after a minute. If Atti could break this, he would have by now.

"She is mine, now," the demon king laughs as the crystal cracks in half. Both pieces fall to the ground, and the cave shakes. The screams from the city get louder, just as I hear a loud roar. *What the hell is that?* Winter lowers her hands almost robotically, still staring at us with an empty look. A witch appears next to the demon king, placing her hand on his shoulder, and he smiles down at her.

"You betraying, little bitch, I will kill you for this!" Atti shouts at the witch, and she shrugs a shoulder.

"You let my daughter die. Taliana should have lived and been your queen!" the witch shouts back, and everything makes a little more sense.

"Trust me; when I get my hands on you, you will beg for the same death as your daughter," Atti promises, and the witch pales a little.

"Winter, Winter, snap out of it," Jaxson shouts, banging on the barrier, and he growls loudly. Winter doesn't move, she doesn't even blink as she stares at us. For a second, I think I see a flicker of blue in her eyes, but it's gone the moment the demon king steps next to her. We need to get him away from her as he must have some way of controlling her. I'm surprised we didn't think of it before. She is his blood.

"You are no kings, you can't even protect your queen," the demon king laughs, and Jaxson growls as I step forward.

"You will die, and I will kill you," I say the words slowly, and the demon looks at me with a smirk that reminds me of my father. I know it's not my father, but it's his body still, it's him still.

"I enjoyed killing your ancestor, he was always the best fighter. Vampires have speed but rarely brains, I believe you have neither. Ah, but children do dream, don't they?" He laughs.

"Things have changed in the years you were locked away," Dabriel says in a clipped tone, his eyes never leaving Winter.

"And your ancestor. I liked him...but he was stupid as well. He tried to kill me and save Elissa," the demon king tells Dabriel.

"You killed your mate, how could you do that?"

"She stole my child, my child!" the demon king spits out. "But it doesn't matter. I have Winter, my grandchild, which is even better," he says with a dark laugh and nods at the dark witch. I watch as he disappears, taking Winter and the witch with him.

"Winter!" Atti shouts, but it's no use. The barrier falls, and the city shakes harder as the ward falls. Screams fill the night as I look at my friends, my brothers.

"We need to save our people and then Winter. She will never forgive us if she comes back to everyone dead or if we kill ourselves trying to get her now," Dabriel tells us all, and we nod, not liking the idea but knowing he is right as we listen to more screams.

"He won't hurt her, he needs her," I tell Jaxson who looks close to shifting. Jaxson looks over at me and nods. "Let's save the city," I say and walk out of the cave with my brothers. Each one of us is broken but willing to fight. First, the city, and then we will save our mate.

CHAPTER 4

DABRIEL

"*I*s that everyone?" I shout after healing a little girl, and her mum nods at me as she holds her close. A bundle of crystals is at her side, and I think back to the crystal trees that the demons burnt down. That's all we have left of the most beautiful and magical trees in the world, just those crystals. I don't hear anyone shout out after a few minutes, but I take the time to look around the infirmary at the witches here. There is only a fraction of the ten thousand that lived in the witches' city. Thousands have died today, and when the barrier dropped, the demon king sent two dragons to kill the rest of the witches and burn the island. It makes sense that he would have creatures like dragons, but knowing of them and seeing them is another matter. We just managed to pull a couple hundred injured witches out of the fires before we had to leave. By now, there will be nothing left of Atlantis. I walk out of the room and look over as two wolves carry a dead witch wrapped in sheets out of the room. *So much death.* The castle is out of control with witches being brought in, and surprisingly, the vampires and wolves are trying to help. There aren't that many witches though, not compared to the ten thousand we knew lived on Atlantis.

"How many?" I ask Wyatt as I walk into the entrance hall where he is talking to a vampire who doesn't look impressed. They are talking in French, which I don't understand a word of, and Wyatt changes the conversation to English when I stop next to them.

"The witches need help, and as your king, I'm saying you will help them. They are mainly women and children, are you that heartless?" Wyatt shouts, and there is silence as the old vampire bows his head and walks away. I'm surprised he didn't use his power to command them, but then he has never been that kind of vampire. Or king.

"Atti called," Wyatt taps the side of his head, not answering my question, but I can tell from the little witches that are here that it is bad. The demons must have killed thousands today, and Winter is gone. How did a day of celebration of Atti becoming the king we knew he was meant to be and mating with Winter, become a day we and the witches will never forget? I follow Wyatt up the stairs, stepping over the witches sitting huddled up, and watch as they bow their heads to us as we pass. They shouldn't bow to us, we have done nothing but let the demon king take our queen. Plus, their city has been destroyed. We go up the four flights of stairs until we get to our rooms that are on one long corridor. Wyatt walks straight to Winter's room, and I shut the doors behind us. Jaxson is sitting on the bed speaking quietly to Freddy, who looks over at Wyatt and nods at him.

"I can't be long as more people need to be healed," I tell Atti who turns to face us with Milo on his shoulder. Milo has some strange, green outfit on that looks made of leather. I bet some doll, somewhere, is missing an outfit. Milo almost makes me smile until I look at his blue skin and memories of Winter come to me.

"We have a way to get Winter back. Well, Milo does," Jaxson says.

"Me," Milo replies and points at his chest.

"Freddy and Milo were talking about the ward around the vampire castle," Atti says, and relief fills me as I see Atti's nod. The annoying little creature who eats Wyatt's Oreos is a demon after all, he might be able to help us. We haven't been able to think of any way to get her back at all. It's seeming hopeless, as we can't fight the demon king while he hides behind his army and the ward.

"Tell me how," I ask Atti.

"I can walk through my blood ward," Milo says and then flies over to sit on my shoulder. He's not making much sense, as he hasn't quite learnt how to put sentences together right yet.

"What Milo means is that he can pull one person through the ward around the vampire castle," Jaxson says, standing up and walking over with Freddy following.

"Who and what's the point? We can't fight the demon king and his army on our own. He could hold a knife to Winter's throat, and we would put our weapons down for her," I say and groan when I realise Freddy is young to be hearing this about someone he loves.

"Winter is going to be okay, right, Uncle J?" Freddy asks Jaxson who puts a hand on his shoulder.

"We are going to get her back, we love her as much as you do. Why don't you go and watch some movies?" Jaxson suggests.

"I'm not a kid, I'm not watching movies when everything is going wrong," Freddy snaps, pushing Jaxson away.

"No, you're not a kid. No kid should have to live what you have gone through already at such a young age. Jaxson only wants to protect you," Wyatt says to him.

"I don't need advice or sympathy from you," Freddy growls out, and Wyatt steps closer, not one bit fazed by his show of aggression.

"Look, Harris and the others are going to need some help sorting out the witches and finding them rooms. Why don't you go and help the beta?" Wyatt suggests, and I see Jaxson nod.

"I will send a message to him. They need help," Jaxson says, and Freddy looks down at the ground before meeting Wyatt's gaze.

"Fine, but save her. I won't forgive you if you don't," he says and walks out of the room.

"The kid is growing up and getting balls to speak to all of us like that," Atti says, making us laugh a little despite the situation.

"Balls? Do humans have balls?" Milo asks, and Atti laughs.

"One day I will explain that, but not now," I tell Milo, who nods with an innocent face. I bet the little demon is winding us up.

"Right, I have an idea for Winter. I'm going; as her mate, I can try to push my magic into her, and hopefully it will snap her out of it. It's the best chance we have, but I'm going to need a distraction," Atti says, making it clear it will be him that goes in after her. I want to suggest I should, but I know it's not what's best for Winter. I have no way of getting her out of his control, whereas Atti does, and I trust him to save her.

"I suggest we take fifty wolves and vampires, and attack the castle," Wyatt says, and we all nod. It's the best way to make a distraction, hopefully the demon king won't take Winter with him.

"I can get fifty witches to appear and take everyone back to the castle after twenty minutes," Atti offers.

"If we time it right, that should be all you and Milo will need to get Winter and get out," Jaxson says, pacing the room.

"She might not come willingly, and you might need to knock her out and bring her here," I say, remembering how she looked at us, how she reacted. She is under his control, and it's going to be a fight. I can't even think about what the demon king might be getting her to do, even in the one day he has had her. If we attack tomorrow, that's two days she will be alone with him and completely under his control. The thought just makes me want to kill him.

"I will save her," Atti promises, his words strong, and I know he will.

"I should go and see the angels; see if they will come here to be safe. I have a feeling the demons will attack them next," I say, but it's more than a feeling. I haven't had any visions; the future seems blocked to me. The last one I had was just a storm. A tornado in a storm, and there was so much fire. I don't know what I was seeing, but I don't want to be around to see that in real life. I still hold on to the vision of Winter and all of us by that lake in the future, but it seems so far away, and I know the future can change in a second, making my visions useless.

"They won't come," Wyatt warns, knowing my race is stubborn, and nothing will make them leave their precious home. They wouldn't want to live with other races, as they see them as inferior.

"Well, at least, I can get some of the healing herbs and bring them here as I can't keep healing everyone," I say, knowing that my old room there has a wall full of jars of herbs laced with my magic.

"Go, brother, and we will plan the attack for tomorrow morning," Jaxson says and pats my shoulder.

"A lift, Atti?" I ask, holding out a hand as Milo flies off my shoulder and goes to sit on top of Winter's bed. Atti grabs my arm and moves us instantly, and when I open my eyes I'm outside the council. The large, white building is so different from the normal houses that line the streets of the village. No humans live in this village, but they do drive past it, believing it's just a field thanks to a witch's ward.

"I'll wait," Atti says and goes to sit on the seats outside as everyone stops moving to stare at us. I'm sure we look a sight with our burnt clothes, and both of us covered in blood and blue dust. I don't care what they think, this is their future if they don't leave. There aren't many angels left to begin with, being that the war with the witches killed so many of us. The idea of even asking the angels to now come and live with those very same witches seems like a disaster, but I won't let them die just because I don't want to ask.

"How dare you bring a witch into the council?" Zadkiel says as he walks down the stairs and smirks at us. Zadkiel's hair is completely shaved off now, and he has decided to wear a royal cloak that I believe our father used to wear. I don't even know where he got it from. At least, he isn't wearing the royal crown; I don't think I would hesitate to kill him if he were.

"I suggest you shut up, brother, before I lose what little control I have and kill you," I tell him. He doesn't move or speak as I open the doors to the council and walk in. My brother was always the coward. My marks appear on my skin without me calling them, because I've been awake so long, and I'm tired. I want my mate safe and need to rest. I don't know how many witches I've healed or demons I've killed in the last day. The council is speaking to each other when I walk in, and only one of them is missing. They might actually listen to me when there are so many of them here.

"The witches' city has fallen. Queen Winter of the witches, wolves, and vampires has been kidnapped, and I'm begging you to move our people to the goddess's castle. It's the only place that is safe and our only chance," I say loudly, and the room goes silent. I look around at the aged angels, seeing the sympathetic look on Lucifer's and Gabriel's faces, but not many others seem that upset about the loss. Thousands of witches and people have died, and they almost look pleased.

"Dabriel, I am sorry for your loss and the loss of the witches' city," Veja says, a dark angel who is old but one of the kinder ones.

"How many died?" Gabriel asks me.

"Thousands, there aren't any more than two thousand witches who escaped," I say, and there's silence around the room. They know how many witches were on that island, they know how a loss like this would be told in history, and that what they say here will be remembered. If the demons killed that many witches, who are powerful, in their own city, the angels will struggle. We don't have the numbers that the witches did, and at least twenty percent of our population are old. We lost a lot of our younger generation in the war.

"Then many demons would have died, and the demon king's army will be smaller. I feel we are safe here," Gabriel says, and dread fills me. They can't be serious. The demon army will be bigger than ever, because he wouldn't have just killed the witches, he would have taken some of them back to the castle and turned them.

"No," I reply, and there's a hushed silence around the room.

"You are thinking with your emotions for your lost mate and not what is best for our people. We have four thousand angels that would not be easy to move without a reason."

"Isn't the death of an entire city reason enough? The witches had ten thousand!" I shout, and it's Melan who speaks.

"Not our city," he says. He must be the oldest angel here, a light angel who has scars from the war, from losing his four sons when the witches killed them. I understand why he would never feel sympathetic to the witches, but this isn't about him and his own desires, this is about the fate of the angels. I don't want my entire race to be destroyed.

"You are all fools," I spit out.

Lucifer stands up. "I side with Dabriel, and I'm taking my family to the goddess's castle. I suggest you do the same and stop being fools," he says and walks around the council and out the doors, nodding at me before he walks out.

"I side with Dabriel. I may believe the demon king army is smaller, but I'm no fool; I know we will not win the fight here. I sincerely hope you choose to follow the rightful king," Gabriel says, shocking me a little, but he nods at me before walking out.

"We will discuss this and wish to have you come back here tomorrow at midnight," Veja says, and I give him a look of shock. I had hoped he would be another to side with me on this, he has a young family.

"It will be too late," I say, knowing if we get Winter back, the demon king will attack the next place he can. I can't tell them we are going after Winter because I cannot trust any of them. They could be working with the demon king, and I wouldn't even know. I won't risk our rescue plan for Winter for anything.

"When our people look back at the history of the biggest war of supernaturals, this will be remembered. It will be remembered how you sat in your chairs and made the biggest mistake that cost lives," I tell them, but not one replies as I turn and walk out of the room. When I get outside the council building, every single angel outside stops and bows their head to me. Atti stands up and walks over, wordlessly placing his hand on my shoulder.

We have our Queen to save.

CHAPTER 5

*D*arkness and snow. Darkness and Winter. Darkness and love. Darkness and life. Which one saves the queen? Which life will end for the queen?

The child-like voice sings through my mind, the sentence keeps repeating and getting louder and louder. I want to scream for it to stop, to stop the song but everything feels cold, and words don't seem to leave my lips when I think them. I blink my eyes open, and there's nothing but blackness. An endless black smoke that fills an empty place. Emptiness and darkness, and I don't know why I'm trying to escape. What is out there in the darkness?

"Wake up, Winter. Winter, you must wake up and wear the crown."

"What crown?" I whisper to the female voice I barely recognise. It's Elissa, my grandmother.

"*Your inheritance. The crown is yours, and you are stronger than him,*" Elissa says, her voice urgent.

"*Who?*" I ask.

"*You're only a quarter demon, Winter. Your humanity is what will save you,*" the voice says. Demon?

"**T**ime to wake up, little princess, I want to talk," a voice says, waking me up from a strange dream that I struggle to remember. Something about humanity and demons. I open my eyes to see a pair of dark red ones watching me; they almost glow in the dimly lit room. *Demon.* The demon king. Everything comes rushing back to me as I lean back in the seat I'm in and try to swallow the fear that climbs up my throat. I glance around the dining room we are sitting in and see the faces of three other people with us. The dining room is a room I've never seen, but the massive windows overlook the vampire gardens, and the library can be seen on the other side through the windows. At least, I know where I am. I look back at the betraying idiots that are sitting at the table. Damn, I'm in trouble. One is an older witch with long, black hair and a grin that is creepy as she watches me too closely. The other two are angels with white wings and look familiar. They both have light purple eyes and cruel expressions. The older one of the two has short hair, whereas the other one has longer hair. I glance down at my hands, one is holding a wine glass, and I don't remember picking it up. I quickly pull my hand away as I look at the table which is set with food and a half-eaten plate in front of me. I rest my hand over one of the knives on the table and the other on my lap. I nearly jump when I see the long dress I'm wearing. It's a corset at the top and has an old-fashioned, lacy skirt. *Damn, the dress is a nightmare on its own.*

"Don't think about it, my princess. I will put you back in your mental cage before you even get a chance to touch me with that knife," the demon king warns. I refuse to even think of him as a relative of mine. We may share blood, but he means nothing to me after what he has done. I turn and look at him, sitting at the head of the table and looking every bit the king he is pretending to be.

"My name is Winter, not princess," I spit out.

"But, you are my princess," he tells me.

"I'm not your anything. I am the queen of three races and soon to be four. When my kings come for me, and they will, you will regret this," I warn him, and his dark laugh fills the room.

"Silly words from a murderer," the witch opposite me says, spitting out the words as I stare into the dark red eyes of the demon king. Other than the slight, grey shade to his gold skin, he still reminds me of Wyatt, as he wears the old vampire king's body. I look up at the crown, the crown which belongs to Wyatt and not him.

"Everyone I have killed has deserved their fate," I turn my gaze away and meet the angry face of the witch.

"My daughter did not deserve you to kill her! She was the queen, you stupid little–" the witch stops shouting as a dagger lands in her neck and blood sprays all over the table. I look away in disgust as her head slams onto the table, and the demon king simply smiles at me.

"No one will insult my princess," he tells me, suggesting he just killed the witch for me. I look back at the witch, her dead eyes facing the windows, and I gather that Taliana must have been her daughter. I understand her anger, her pain, and she died because of it.

"She didn't deserve this," I mutter, and the angel with no hair replies.

"Yes, she did, beautiful one," he says, and I glare at him.

"Does your king know you're here?" I ask, and he slams his hand on the table, making me jump.

"I will be king," he says, and I just laugh.

"You will regret this, being here," I say to the angel who looks seconds away from trying to kill me before looking at the dead witch's body out of the corner of his eye.

"Do you know your father said those words as one of my demons killed him?" the demon king tells me.

"What?" I ask quietly, shock shaking me to my core. My father died in a car accident, or that's what I was told happened. I doubt my mum would have lied to me about that.

"Your father said those last words as my demons tortured him to death. It was a shame he wouldn't speak a word about where you were. He died protecting you from me, and yet, here you are," he says, leaning toward me and resting his head on his joined hands.

"It was a car accident," I spit out, not believing a word that comes from him. He only chuckles and leans back in his seat, linking his hands together.

"No, it wasn't, but he was only a silly human

that my daughter thought would be safe to love," he says.

"He was not a silly human. He was my father and a brave man," I say, standing up and calling my power. The second it leaves me and releases a blue wave, the angels in the room go flying along with the dead witch body, which I almost regret doing. The demon king just watches me as I look at him, the blue wave not bothering him one bit as he lifts a hand and makes his own ward.

"They say you were once human and innocent. I see that is no longer true of you," the angel with shaved hair says after he flies over, landing next to me. I lift the knife off the table and hold it in front of me as I push the chair out of the way, walking backwards.

"So, beautiful, I know why my brother liked you now. I know why he is going to die for you," the angel comments as he reaches a hand out to me, but I whack it away with the knife, cutting him, and turn, running for the door. Dabriel's brother is here, and it makes sense why the angel looks familiar. My mind runs over the fact it means the angels must be working with the demon king. *I need to escape*. Just as I open the massive hall doors, a haunting dark laugh fills my ears. Blackness fills my eyes as everything disappears, and I feel myself drop the knife.

"And I only wanted a nice family dinner, what a shame," I hear the demon king taunt as blackness takes over my eyes.

CHAPTER 6

"*Elissa, run,*" *a man roars as I open my eyes and see the entrance hall to the castle. Pieces of stone and dust fall from the ceiling near me, but I can see the destruction surrounding me. I turn and just see the back of Elissa, running up the steps of the castle. The castle is old and in ruins as one wall is on fire and another is in crumbles. The smoke in the room just floats around the white dress I'm wearing, the sparks coming off the wall of fire should burn me, but they don't. I can't even feel the heat from the room; if anything, it still feels cold.*

"*You and I then, boy,*" *the familiar voice of the demon king says, and I turn to see the voice coming from an attractive, middle-aged man. The man has a long, black cloak on and dark black hair. He stands holding a sword at his side, and at his feet is the dead body of Atti's ancestor, the first* witch. I watch as he holds the blood-covered sword up at his side, blood dripping onto the stone floor.

"Whatever happens here today, she is safe. She will live, and her child will finish this war. She will finish you," the voice of the first vampire, Wyatt's ancestor, says as he holds his own sword in the air. They don't say any more words as the demon king rushes forward and attacks him, their swords clashing together, and the force nearly springing them both backwards. I try to move as they fight, as I know the ending to this vision already, he will die. Both are fast, but the demon king is better, it's clear with every hit and swing of his sword. The demon king hits the vampire ancestor in his side, and he falls a little, giving the demon king the second he needs to shove his sword straight through his heart.

"No," I breathe out, but no sound comes from my lips, and the world is silent for a second before the vampire ancestor's pale face has black lines crawling over it, and he collapses on the floor.

"All but children in a game I've played for many, many years," the demon king says, his tone almost soft as he speaks to the two bodies on the floor. He steps over the witch and walks up the stairs, going after Elissa. I turn slightly to the left and see a woman walk in, her long, white cloak dotted with blood. She lowers the hood, and shock fills me when, for a second, I think it's Elissa, but it's not. It's Demtra, but they look so alike, the only difference is the hair and eyes. I met her *once when I died, and I thought it was Elissa, but it never was. Demtra looks straight at me, her green eyes staring straight through me.*

"They did not fall so that you would fall, Queen Winter. Only you can stop this, you and your mates," she then gestures to the bodies on the floor, "their last children if this is not stopped. Win the war, Queen Winter, win the war, win the war..." Demtra says in my mind, and the sentence repeats again and again in my mind as she walks up the stairs.

I shoot up in bed, feeling a hand shaking my shoulder, and open my eyes to see Atti leaning over me, relief spread across his handsome face before he takes my face in his hands and kisses me. I throw myself into the kiss, letting him pull me closer. I break away and just stare up at him, seeing his stormy, grey eyes that almost glow. He has a cloak on, his hood up, so I can't see his blond hair, but I lift my hand and place it on his cheek under the hood.

"Atti," I whisper, seeing him close his eyes and pull me close. The bond between us is clear when I'm in his arms, my back almost tingles, reminding me of my marks and Atti's, which I haven't seen yet.

"We have to leave," Milo's voice comes from near us, and I break away from Atti to look over at the door, where Milo is hovering in the air. Milo has a strange, green outfit on and a green sash holding his white hair up. It's such a relief to see them both, but as I look around, I have a feeling we aren't out of danger yet.

"Milo, Atti, how are you here?" I ask, looking around the bedroom I'm in and down at the black dress I'm still wearing. I'm still in the vampire castle; how am I not under his control, and where is he?

"Milo can pull people through demon wards, now we have to go. The distraction isn't going to be long," Atti tells me and pulls me off the bed. A wave of dizziness hits me as I stand up, and I can feel the demon king in my mind, only a little bit. It's like a dark stain.

"Wait . . . how did you?" I ask Atti, pulling his hand to stop us walking across the room.

"Make you not, well, controlled? I just flooded your system with my magic, mates can do that. You might feel a little–" Atti says, and I interrupt him.

"Dizzy?" I ask, resting on his shoulder, and he nods.

"Can you run?" he asks me. I stand straighter and remember everything I have to fight for. This isn't the time to be weak, I don't have time for that.

"Yes," I reply, and Atti links our hands as we run out of the room. Milo lands on my shoulder. I smile at him, and he rests his head next to mine as we stop at the end of the corridor, and Atti looks around it before we start running down the next one.

"Glad you safe," Milo says quietly and lightly kisses the side of my head.

"Me too, and thank you for saving me. I will always be thankful," I tell him quietly, and Atti smiles at me before we stop at the end of another corridor. Atti places a finger on his lips as he looks around the edge of the wall and then nods at me, tugging on my hand. We run down familiar-looking corridors, and Atti has to catch me when I trip on the lacy dress, ripping it. I pick some of the dress up as we get outside, and I hear the sound of screaming in the background. When the ground shakes, and the blast is strong enough to shake the castle, I know Jaxson is near. Worry fills me from the idea of him fighting the demon king, but I trust my mates to have made a plan.

"Jaxson?" I ask Atti as we run down the main court area and towards the large walls that enclose the castle. It's surprising how there isn't anyone here, not a single person or demon around. I think back to the humans that used to live here, how they never really had a chance to truly live, to be free and are most likely dead or demons now. I'm not sure which fate would have been better for them. An awful, groaning noise comes from next to us as we run, and I look to the left of Atti to see two demons running at us. They look horrible, their grey skin falling off their faces, and the smell from them can't be missed.

"Jaxson is making the distraction," Atti tells me and pushes me behind him as he raises his hands, and a large stream of fire leaves his hands. I look around him to see two piles of blue dust, and then we are running again before I can look at or say anything. In some ways, killing them is putting them to rest. Or that's what I have to keep telling myself.

"We need to jump, can you do that?" Atti asks me, and I look up at the big wall and the blue ward that is just on the other side. Milo starts flying up as I watch and take a few steps back.

"Yes," I say remembering my training with Leigha. She would kick my ass if I don't jump this. All that training is finally becoming useful, and I could just see her smirking at me if I told her she was right.

"One, two, three," Atti says, and I run next to him, jumping at the same time and pushing as much as I can to make the jump. I fly through the air and just manage to hit the top, catching my hands on the stone and hanging off the edge. My hands scrape across the sharp stone, and it cuts my fingers, my blood making it harder to hold on as the cold wind pushes me to the side. I look up, just as it starts to snow, it's falling thickly from the sky. I try to pull myself up, but the stupid dress catches on the stone and stops me from using my legs to help. These old dresses are not meant for climbing. Atti lands after me, pulls himself up, and reaches down to lift me up only seconds later. He pulls me to his chest, and I gently press my lips to his.

"My mate," I say softly, and he presses his forehead into mine. Atti lifts my cut hands and wipes his thumb across the cuts, which are slowly healing on their own. My teeth extend, but I don't feel hungry, which only makes me feel sick. I must have been fed or fed on someone while I was here. It's the only thing that makes sense.

"Hey, don't leave me and disappear into your thoughts. I missed you, and whatever it is you're worried about, we will sort it," he tells me, and I look up at him.

"I missed you, too," I whisper, and he kisses my forehead before he steps away, our moment gone as we both walk over to the dark blue ward. The ward is thick, almost stopping you from seeing the other side and the forest behind it.

"You touch and push," Milo tells me as he flies over, and Atti holds out his hand to Milo.

"You think I can walk through the ward?" I ask Milo, who nods his little head, making his hair bounce up and down.

"Demon, you," he tells me, and I nod back, understanding what he means. I should be able to do this because it's part of who I am. If the demon king can use that small part of me to control me, then I should be able to use it, too. I step forward at the same time Milo pulls Atti through the ward. I push my hands against it, feeling it pushing back like a sponge, but the more I push the further I can walk. I push and hold my breath, closing my eyes as I step through the ward. I gasp for air when I finally break through the other side, and I hear a loud shout.

"No!" the demon king's roar seems to echo around my mind, and I hold my hands over my ears as darkness starts spreading in my eyes. My power starts rising, and I scream as I push it away, refusing to let it hurt anyone. Especially not my mate.

"Atti," I whisper, feeling his hands picking me up and then the feeling of us moving, seconds before everything disappears into a familiar darkness.

CHAPTER 7

"Winter," a familiar voice says as a hand strokes my cheek, and I open my eyes to see my angel leaning over me. Dabriel watches me closely, his hair falling around his face and his marks glowing ever so slightly all over his skin. I've never spent a lot of time looking over each mark, seeing how they all resemble shapes, and they are difficult to look at for too long as it hurts your eyes. It's kind of like looking at the sun. Dabriel has a white shirt on and jeans, but they are crinkled, and he looks tired. I look down to see I'm wearing the stupid black dress still, and I'm lying on top of the covers of my bed at the goddess's castle. The bedroom is such a comfort to see, as much as being with one of my mates.

"Dab," I say, sitting up, and he pulls me to him with a contented groan. I wrap my arms around his neck and kiss his cheek, waiting only a second for him to turn his head and fully kiss me. I moan as he slides his hands into my hair, and his tongue gently wrestles with my own. This is everything, being here with him and being safe.

"You're awake, lass," Jaxson says from somewhere nearby, and Dabriel breaks away from the kiss, leaning back, so I can see Jaxson as he walks into the room. Jaxson looks tired, but so determined, as he walks over to me and leans down, pulling me off the bed and into a hug. I wrap my legs around his waist as he kisses me fast, then breaks away.

"I fucking missed you, don't do that again. I can't keep losing you like this," he tells me. I run my hand over his beard that needs shaving and the messy hair that falls slightly into his face. He looks tired but still has the wild side to him, the side that makes him the very wolf I know he is.

"It's not like I chose a family reunion, Jaxson," I say, wriggling out of his arms, and he sighs as he lets me go. "How did the distraction go?" I ask him, looking him over for any injuries but not seeing any.

"I decided the best way to get his attention was

to destroy half the castle, so I caused an earthquake and brought down the left side of the castle," Jaxson says with a shrug like it was nothing when I bet that was some hell of a show of power. "The demons attacked, and we held them off, until the demon king got there. I went to fight him when he realised you had gone, and then the witches came and used their power to portal everyone out," Jaxson tells me. I bet the demon king was mad.

"What happened to you? How could he take power over you, make you almost a zombie?" he asks me gently.

"He controlled me somehow; he got into my head and made everything go black."

"Do you know about the witches?" Dabriel asks me gently, and I shake my head. I only remember the witch the demon king killed at that messed-up dinner. There isn't anything else, just blackness, and every time I try to think about it, it seems to slip away from my thoughts.

"Winter, he used you to destroy the crystal ward that protected the witches' city. Then he brought his dragons in, and the island is destroyed."

"Dragons? He used me?" I ask, shock making me feel sick.

"Yes, but it wasn't your fault."

"How many witches survived the attack?" I ask, and Jaxson hesitates before he tells me.

"About three thousand, maybe less as a lot are injured still," he says, and I know that means thousands died in the witches' city. A city full of people I'm meant to protect as I'm their queen, and instead, I let the demon king use me to destroy the ward that protected them.

"It's not your fault, you know that?" Dabriel asks me, and I just look away. There's silence between us all as I guess they don't know what to say to me. It is my fault no matter what they say. I should have done something, fought more or tried to wake myself up. If I hadn't been stupid in the first place, the demon king wouldn't have even escaped.

"What do you remember, Winter? Anything you could tell us could help at this point." Dabriel asks me, trying to give me a way to be useful.

"I don't remember much, only bits. I remember a dinner, and two angels were there with a witch," I say but turn to talk to Dabriel more. I hate that I have to tell him about his brothers. No matter the fact I know he doesn't get along with them, this is more than just sibling fights. No, this means his family betrayed him, and I know he will never forgive them for it.

"What angels?" Dabriel asks me, sliding off the bed, his wings gently fluttering at the side of him.

"They were your brothers, they told me," I tell him gently, and he frowns, standing up. I won't tell him what else they said to me or about him dying, I would never let that happen. I would never let any one of my mates die for me.

"And they are working with the demon king. It wouldn't surprise me to know the whole council is," he says, coming over and kissing my forehead. I wrap an arm around his waist, feeling his one wing almost holding me to him. I wonder if he even notices he is doing it. I can't help but gently guide my hand over his wing, and I feel him gently shiver.

"I'm happy you're safe and here, but I must go and speak with Lucifer. If the angels are working with them, we are not as safe as I would like," he tells me, and I nod. I get it, being the royals we are means we don't have a lot of time to celebrate them saving me. Dabriel walks out the door, holding it open as Freddy runs in and tackles me in a hug. I take a deep breath as the kid almost suffocates me with his strong arms.

"You're back," he says, happily squeezing me, and I hold him close.

"I am, where is Wyatt?" I ask Jaxson over Freddy's head.

"We are having problems with the witches and vampires, there is a fight going on, or he would be here. He saw you before Atti, and he had to go and deal with the problems," he says, and it's not surprising, knowing that my mates would have brought the surviving witches here. Now, we are trying to make vampires, witches, and wolves live together after hating each other for so long. There is always going to be arguments, but I know this is the best thing for us. This castle is the safest place.

"Let's go then," I say, letting go of Freddy and letting Jaxson take my hand as he leads us out of the bedroom.

"Go and find Katy and Harris will you, Freds? They will want to know Winter is back," Jaxson asks Freddy when we get outside my bedroom. Freddy gives Jaxson a grumpy look before sighing.

"Fine," Freddy says and runs down the corridor in the opposite direction. I look up at Jaxson as he leads us out of the corridor that has our rooms, and I hear the shouting the moment we get to the top of the stairs. I listen to the arguments as we walk down the four flights of stairs and past many witches, wolves, and vampires that are leaning over the bannister and watching. Many turn and look at me with wide eyes that have a range of respect, kindness and—what's worse—fear.

"Ils ne restent pas ici, ni les sorcières," I hear some man shout, his French words I don't understand leading me to guess he is one of the vampires.

"I don't want to be around stupid old vampires anyway. At least us witches aren't cruel, evil people," I hear shouted back to whatever the man shouted in French. I come down the stairs just in time to see Atti hold a witch against the wall by his neck, while Wyatt lifts another older-looking vampire off the ground by his coat, his feet hanging off the ground.

"What the hell is going on?" I ask, and the room goes silent. Wyatt drops the vampire at the same time that Atti lets go of his man, they both smile over at me. *Atti and Wyatt both look stressed even with the smiles.* That's the only thought that comes to mind as I rest my eyes on them. Atti has his cloak on, the black contrasts against his wavy, blonde hair and his grey eyes light up as I smile at him. Wyatt draws my attention the most right now, it feels like forever since I've seen him. I let my eyes drop down his body, seeing the tight trousers and button down white shirt he has on, showing off his impressive body. His dark, almost bottomless, brown eyes watch me, and I think he is feeling the same as me. The urge to be close to my mate is hard to resist, even with the number of eyes on us. It's almost funny the looks of happiness they give me, like they weren't just stopping a fight, or Wyatt wasn't holding a vampire up by his neck. The vampire on the floor coughs and moves away, but I'm kind of proud of Wyatt, he could have just used his compulsion on the vampire and made him stop. Instead, he was trying to be reasonable, well as reasonable as a vampire prince who just got his mate back can get, that is.

"Nothing we can't deal with," Wyatt says, his eyes drifting over me and finally landing on my eyes. I take a step closer to him and trip, almost falling, but Jaxson slides an arm around my waist and stops me. I clear my throat and look down, seeing nothing. I just tripped on air in front of lots of people, damn it.

"Supernaturals are not meant to live together, this is wrong," the witch with light blond hair, who

Atti was holding, says as he stands up and shakes his head at me. Jaxson's loud growl is enough to make him stay quiet and not comment on whatever he is thinking. I know I don't have many fans with the witches, not after what I did to their city, but they don't seem to look at me with hate like I expected them to. No, they seem to only have fear in their eyes as they stare at the vampires and wolves. I glance around at the five female witches with their hoods down, bundled together on one side and then to the ten or so vampires huddled closely together. The wolves are grouped together by the door. The space between them is huge.

"Everyone, listen!" I shout, and the crowd of witches, vampires, and wolves turn to look at me. I take a deep breath, knowing I need to say this and then spend time figuring out everything else.

"The demon king has an army, a massive army. I saw them. He has thousands and thousands of soldiers that will kill anything in their way, and they have the weapons to kill us. He won't stop until we are all dead: witch, vampire, wolf, or angel. It doesn't matter to him," I tell them, the fear shining in their eyes as they watch me.

"Isn't he your grandfather? You brought down

the ward and let the dragons in!" a female witch says and steps forward.

"You're right, he is. He has also killed all my blood relatives. He has killed because he is insane, and his thirst for power is out of control. I can only say I'm truly sorry for the ward, for letting him take control of my mind and not figuring out he has that power."

"How do we know you won't flip and start attacking us?" an older, French vampire asks, watching me with his hand on a sword strapped to his side.

"If you attack her, if anyone attacks my queen, I will personally rip you to pieces," Jaxson growls out, and the vampire looks down. I place my hand on Jaxson's shoulder and step away from him.

"The demon king can't come here, and he can only control me when he is close. I understand your fear, I feel it, too. I have family here, and you are my people. I won't stop until he is back in hell, where he belongs. You may not trust me, or some of you may hate me for everything I've done. It doesn't matter; at the end of the day, war is coming. In war, you will see I side with you. I was human once, but I never felt right. I felt lost, and now, being here is home," I say, and several of the supernaturals all look at each other.

"Our queen is right, we are at war, and squabbling like children over race is not going to win us a war that will save our children. Save our mates," Atti shouts into the room and then walks over to my side.

"There has never been a threat like this, there has never been a war like this. We will all die if we don't work together, our children will die. There isn't a choice here. We fight or we die. You make your choice and spread the word. Those who want to fight, meet me and the other kings in the training rooms in the morning. Those who don't or won't, stay out of our way, or I will kill you myself," Wyatt shouts, and his voice echoes around the room as whispers follow. I watch as he walks over to me, sliding his hands over my cheeks and kissing me.

"We will win this for you," he tells me, and lets go, dropping to his one knee in front of me and bowing his head. Jaxson and Atti mimic his actions, and so do all the other people in the room, each one of them kneeling and bowing their heads. I look over to see Alex standing near the door, her arms crossed, and she winks at me before bowing herself.

"We will win this war, and I will kill the demon

king. It's what I'm destined to do. It's what my grandmother, my great aunt, her mates, and my parents died for. I will fight for us all," I say, my words echoing as I leave out the most important part of the prophecy, that someone will die, and I'm going to make sure it's me. No one else is dying for me.

CHAPTER 8

"*W*hat the hell are you wearing?" Alex asks as she walks over to me after everyone else has walked away other than my mates. She pulls me into a tight hug, and I just don't move except to hold her back. It feels like a long time since I hugged my best friend.

"Other than looking like a weird, goth princess, are you okay?" she whispers to me, the words only meant for me to hear.

"I'm good, just…it was like sleeping and having no control. I don't remember much, and it's best I don't," I tell her quietly, and she lets go. Memories of thousands of dead, demon soldiers, the smell of death, and the demon king's glowing red eyes will haunt me for years. I have trouble pushing them out of my mind as I try to focus on my best friend. Alex looks amazing as usual, with her red hair down and wearing some kind of leather leggings that stick to her and a baggy white top that hangs off of one shoulder.

"I have something I need to talk to you about," she tells me, and I frown wondering what when I see Harris and Katy running into the room, followed by Anna holding baby Marie in her arms. Marie looks so much older, which I know babies grow quickly, but it's still a sight to see. It's Anna's haunted eyes that hold my attention as I watch them come come closer.

"Winter!" Katy shouts and hugs me. "What on earth are you wearing? I want to say you look good, but err..." Katy says as she lets go.

"I know, right? It's awful, that dress should have burnt in the eighteen hundreds and never made it this far," Alex says, both of them eyeing my awful dress. *Hey, it's not like I disagree with them.*

"Win, shit, I was worried about you," Harris says, and he wraps his giant arms around me.

"I'm good," I say as he moves away.

He nods, "I let you down, My Queen, and–"

"Don't start that stuff, or I will start feeling

guilty, too," Leigha's sharp voice comes from behind me, and I turn to see her push her way through my mates, and she gives me a small smile.

"Back from the demon den, then?"

"Did you miss me, army brat?"

"In training, I did," she smirks, and Harris walks over to her, wrapping an arm around her waist and kissing the side of her head. Her red cheeks and small smile she gives him is enough proof to me that she loves him. And the fact that no one seems shocked by their actions.

"I heard what happened with Esta. What she did," Anna says softly next to me, and I turn to look at her. Despite her soft tone, her eyes have anger in them. Anna's pale complexion matches her blonde hair, which is up in a bun, and the casual clothes she has on. Marie has a Babygro on, and the wavy, blonde hair is all I can see as Anna holds Marie on her shoulder.

"Esta," Anna says her name in anger, and the silence in response to her words is enough to know everyone has spoken about it. Someone has told her, and in a way, I'm glad it's not me that has to.

"She told me she killed Fergus, just before she died," I reply, and she nods, knowing this.

"And you gave her forgiveness," Anna says, her tone filled with judgement.

"I had little choice. I gave her my forgiveness, not yours, not the pack's, and not Jaxson's. I showed kindness in front of thousands of witches that watched me as I took their throne. The one I took from a cruel witch, and they needed to see I'm different. I couldn't be cruel to someone who died for me, not in their last moment. What she did was because of her love for Jaxson and her need to be with him. In the end, I felt sorry for her," I tell Anna, and there's silence as we stare at each other.

"You're my queen, my friend, but she took my mate. I do understand your decision, and it's your kindness that led you to that choice. I hate her for what she did, that she was at the birth of Fergus's child, and that she pretended to be my friend. I hate her and hope she rots in hell for her crimes. I wish she was still alive, so I could kill her myself," Anna spits out, and her eyes start glowing and only stop as Marie cries a little. She hushes Marie gently and pats her back.

"Do you hate me?" I ask quietly, and she looks down at her baby and back to me.

"No. I understand. Winter . . . win this war for

us, for Marie, and honour Fergus's memory that way," she says firmly and waits for my nod before she walks away. Leigha pats my shoulder as she passes with Harris and Katy following her. I wait until they all walk away before I look up at Jaxson who walks to my side.

"I understand what you did, Winter. You're a better person than me, I would have told her to rot in hell before killing the bitch, myself. But she was still pack, and you acted like a shifter queen who lost a pack mate, no matter the circumstances," Jaxson tells me, his voice dripping with anger as I look up at him.

"Thank you." I nod, and he pulls me into his arms.

"Queen Winter, King Jaxson, King Wyatt, and King Atticus," the voice pauses for a moment,. "I don't know who you are," Lucifer says, looking at Alex as he walks over to us and bows low.

Alex and I share a look, there are way too many attractive men in this room, and I know she is thinking the same thing.

"Just Alex. I don't need all that fuss, hot stuff," Alex says, and I laugh a little as Lucifer gives her a strange look.

"Hot stuff? Am I on fire?" he asks and pats down his black shirt making Alex laugh.

"No, it's a human saying."

"A very strange one, indeed," Lucifer says and looks at me, "Queen Winter—" he starts to say, and I interrupt him.

"Lucifer, you supported my mate when few others did and showed me memories I will remember forever as they are all I have of my parents, so we are friends. Just "Winter" please, I'm your friend first," I say, and he nods with a small smile.

"I wish to look into your mind, Queen Winter. I can see your past these last few days and then convince the angels that Zadkiel is working with our enemy. I doubt the council truly knows, and I want to give the angels, my people, the best chance I can," Lucifer says and holds out a hand as Dabriel comes into the room with another angel I've never seen. He nods at me as he continues speaking to the angel while they walk over. I slide my hand into Lucifer's and watch as he glows with his black symbols. I expect him to show me, but he doesn't, I watch as his black eyes disappear back to normal, purple ones. When I think about it, I'm glad he doesn't show me, I don't need any more memories to have nightmares about.

"I could see the meal with Zadkiel and Govan, and little bits of the army he has," Lucifer says, reminding me of the brief image I have of Paris and the dead army he has inside it. It's like a ticking time bomb, waiting to destroy the world. They could so easily. A memory flitters through my mind of the demon king shouting that the humans keep dying as the demons try to take over them. That thousands are dying all the time, and thousands of humans keep hiding from him in the city.

"We should go to the angels, all of us. A united front," I say, and there's silence as Dabriel walks over to me.

"No fucking way," Jaxson snaps out.

"You may be my mate, but you don't control me. Don't speak to me like that, Jax," I snap back, and he growls lightly.

"I lost you, I fucking lost you, and you expect me to let you go anywhere near him again?" Jaxson says, and my anger disappears when I realise his reaction is pure fear of losing me again, nothing more.

"Jax, I'm here now, and what happened before, won't happen again. He chose a time when we were celebrating winning the crown and mating to Atti because we were all distracted. Nothing is going to distract us again," I say and look over at Wyatt and Atti as they step closer.

"I'm not taking you out of this castle, Winter. The demon king could take control of you again, and we can't risk him using you to get here. The winter solstice is in two weeks. He is coming then, and we have no way of preventing him from taking over your mind," Dabriel says gently, making me turn to look at him as he slides a comforting hand down my arm.

"How about we go, and I stay next to Atti the whole time? He can pull me away the second anything happens, but it's unlikely the demon king will be there. I know it's a risk, but I feel like I need to be there," I try to reason.

"Atti?" I ask when no one responds, and he looks down at me as he moves in front of me. Atti places his hand on my cheek, and I rest my head into it.

"You don't leave my side?" he asks, almost in a whisper, fear coating his eyes, and I nod.

"Fine, we will go tonight," he says.

"Someone needs to go and get my mum. The wolves protecting her won't be enough if the demon king finds her. He must be furious I'm gone. I need her here," I tell them all.

"I will send a witch, Leigha, and Drake to get her. Between them, they will be able to safely get her here," Atti says and kisses my cheek before walking off.

CHAPTER 9

"I should go and get changed. Alex?" I ask her, and she walks over, linking her arm in mine as we walk away from them all, and I feel them watching me. My back almost tingles with the knowledge that all my mates are watching me, and I turn my head to see them. They look every bit as powerful as I know they are. But there's more than that, I feel nothing but love as I meet each of their eyes and give them a little smile. I haven't even seen what my new mark looks like since I mated with Atti, and all I want is to see it. We walk up the stairs, and instead of walking to my corridor, I walk down the opposite one.

"Where are we going?" Alex asks me.

"To see the crystal, I need to know something," I tell her, and she nods.

"Why didn't you tell your mates?"

"I need to speak with it alone. They won't let me touch it after last time, and I can't really explain this feeling I have. I think the crystal is somehow in my dreams, the child-like voice I always hear; I think it is the crystal," I tell her as we stop and open the doors to the tower. I'm surprised no one is guarding it like they should be, but I make a mental note to sort something out later. I shut the doors behind us and stop on the bottom step of the stairs.

"Can I be alone?" I ask her, and she looks behind me up the stairs and meets my eyes.

"I trust you," she says simply, and I know there isn't much more that is needed to be said. I climb up the dozens of stairs of the tower and feel the crystal calling to me before I even see it. The crystal is as huge as I remember it being, it lightly glows, and I look around the room to see someone has drawn on the walls, and there are tools on the floor. It looks like they planned to put windows in here, and the very thought makes me happy. People should be able to see the beautiful light from the crystal. I walk over, whispering quietly to it.

"Hello. I know this may seem weird. Okay, it is

weird that I'm talking to a giant crystal, but I know you're alive in here. I feel it. You sing to me, just like the crystal trees in the witches' city. You have been in my dreams and helping me, is that true?"

I place my hands on the crystal, seeing the millions of little lights inside swirl around and then rush at the place my hands are, before the light shines so brightly that I can't see anything for a second.

"Winter," the child-like voice says as I open my eyes, and the little lights from the crystal have formed into a ball in the middle. I look only for a second before the loud, sorrow-filled song fills my mind:

C*hild of Winter . . .*
Child of demons . . .
Child of the ancient ones.

A child planned to rule, a child planned to save.

For all children grow to love, to mourn, but only the child of death will pay the ultimate price. A price for love, for the world.

Death and sorrow, death and love, death and wishes for change will never be sought. The prophecy tells the truth, as much as time will pass.

Blood will fall, blood will fall, blood will fall…

T he song drifts off as my hands start to burn on the crystal, but I don't move my hands away.

"I understand, I know it's my life that must be given to save everyone," I whisper and only a small whisper responds to me.

"You will understand at the final choice."

I pull my hands away, the ball of light breaking into millions of little lights inside the crystal, and the power I felt in the room seems to have disappeared. I look down at my slightly burnt hands as they heal and then back to the crystal, feeling like I'm missing something. Like it knows something that I don't.

I shut the door to my room after leaving the tower with Alex, and she hasn't said a word, the confused look on my face likely says it all. I instantly start pulling the dress off, and when it falls to the ground, I look at my back in the mirror. Despite my underwear being in the way a little, it's one hell of a massive mark all down my back. The brave wolf at the bottom, the strong phoenix next, then Atti's beautiful tree is in the middle of the delicate wings. My heart hurts when I think of the trees in the witches' city, how they are lost to us for the time being. I hope when we get the city back, and we will, we can re-grow them. Their beautiful songs play through my head a million times as I just stare at my reflection. So much has been lost, and so much more is going to be lost. How can I be strong enough to save everyone? To do what I need to?

"Here," Alex says, coming over and handing me some jeans and a black top, snapping me out of my thoughts.

"Your mating marks are beautiful," she tells me as I pull the clothes on.

"Thank you. They are," I reply as I pick the awful dress up and walk over to the fireplace. I chuck it in and look around until I find some matches, before setting the damn thing on fire.

"It looks better on fire." Alex chuckles as she stands next to me, and we watch the fire burn the black material. Even the awful smell from the burning fabric doesn't make me move. I want to watch it burn.

"What did the crystal say?"

"Nothing I didn't already know. I think it's alive," I reply.

"That's . . . well, I would say crazy, but we live in a crazy world."

"A crazy, dangerous world," I reply, and she nods at me before sitting on the end of my bed and looking down at the ground. Alex never makes much sound as she cries, I know her too well. Alex never cries, it's just not her way, but the rare times I've seen her cry, it's been for a bad reason, and worry fills me. Nothing else can be wrong, not with my best friend, too.

"What's wrong?" I ask, keeping the fear out my voice as I walk over and sit next to her.

"I know it's the worst timing, the worst thing that could have happened right now, and I swear we were being safe, but it happened," she whispers after a long silence. Confusion fills me as I look at her, I have no idea where she is going with this.

"What happened? Whatever it is, I'll cover for you. If it's hiding a body or helping you kill some-one, I will, no questions asked," I say, making her laugh a little as she shakes her head at me. I watch her closely as I take her hand. She shocks me to my core as she places her other hand on her stomach, and I figure out what is going on before she even says it.

"I'm pregnant," she whispers, and I sit back in shock, keeping hold of her hand. Alex is pregnant.

"Oh, wow. I didn't expect that," I mutter, my eyes going from her face to her stomach and back again.

"I know, but it happened, and I couldn't be more scared. Every time I close my eyes, fear just fills me. I can't shake the powerless feeling I have," she admits.

"Why are you scared? You will make a wonderful mother," I ask her, knowing for certain she will.

"We are at war Winter. We could die, and anything that happens to me, happens to my baby. I love her or him already, I know it's early to feel this way, but I do. I would do anything to save my baby."

"No, we won't die. You will not die, and you will have this baby. He will not win this time. I will fight for our freedom, our lives. The lives of our future," I say and nod my head towards her stomach. Any doubt I had about winning this war, about giving my life up slips away as I think about Alex's baby.

"I want to be at your side, fighting, but Drake

won't have it, and I can't help but agree with him. Vampire pregnancies are so rare, and everyone I've asked says they are difficult to carry for half-turned like me," she says, and it's not surprising. I know about the low birth rate all supernaturals have.

"Someone will need to be with the women and children who can't fight. Someone needs to be helping the injured, and that's where you're going to be," I say, and she hugs me. Neither of us moves for a long time, just holding each other and my mind running over the idea of Alex and a baby.

"I can't wait to meet her or him," I whisper to her in the quiet room, only the sound of the fire crackling in the background to listen to.

"Winter, come now," Leigha bursts into the room, blood pouring down the side of her head. Her clothes are ripped in various places, and when I see the blue dust on her, panic fills me.

"Leigha what happened?" I ask, standing up.

At the same time, Alex asks, "Where's Drake? Where's our mum?"

"We'd just gotten to your mum, and demons came. There were so many, we barely got away. I think they were waiting for us, for anyone to come. Drake and your mum are badly injured," Leigha tells us as we run down the corridor and down the stairs. Alex makes a strangled sound, and everything goes blurry as I run after Leigha.

"No, no, no," Alex mutters, wiping her eyes as we follow Leigha through the castle and run past many people who stop and stare. Leigha slams the door of a room open. It's full of beds, and I see Dabriel first as he is glowing.

"Winter," I hear someone say, but everything seems slow as I walk over to Dabriel and see my mum on the bed in front of him. There are three long cuts in the front of her top, and there is blood everywhere as Dabriel tries to heal her. I look over at the two silver swords at the side of the bed, covered in blood and back to my mum.

"Mum?" I ask, taking her hand, but she is unconscious. I look over to see another light angel I don't know, glowing lighter than Dabriel, and watch as he pulls two daggers out of Drake's stomach as Alex leans over him. Next to him is a female light witch, three daggers in her arm, and she winces as she pulls them out.

"Winter, I can't. I'm sorry, but the cuts are laced with the same poison that killed Atti's mother, and your mother is too human to survive this," Dabriel says quietly, his purple eyes locking on mine as he gives me the news I knew from the moment I saw my mum. I can't lose her, too. This cannot be happening. I'm so stupid, I should have demanded she come here, no matter what she wanted.

"No!" I shout, pushing him out of the way as he removes his hands, and my mum looks up at me as her eyes slowly open. I push her grey hair out of her face, wincing when I leave a trail of blood on her cheek from my hands.

"Alex, come and say goodbye," I hear Dabriel say, and the sound of Alex's crying fills the room.

"Go say goodbye to your mother. I'm okay, Alex," I hear Drake say, and then I hear her move closer as I stare into my mum's eyes. I don't look away.

"I love you both, you know that?" she whispers out, her breaths sounding slower and slower as I brush some hair out of her eyes.

"I love you, too, mum, please don't leave me," Alex begs as she grips her hand.

"Sing for me, Winter, I love your singing," she mumbles, and I nod, wiping my eyes. I don't know what to sing as I open my mouth, and then a song fills my mind. A song she used to sing to me as a child.

"Blue, blue rose, dancing in the snow. Oh blue, blue rose you have come to say Winter has finally come. Winter brings

the cold but the warmth along, too. I can hear the snow fall-
ing, I can hear the foxes sleeping, and I can hear the sun
setting as Winter comes . . . as the snow falls, and all is clear
. . . "

"Winter, save us. Save us all, and I'm so proud of you both," she says as I stop singing. Blood flows out of her mouth, before her hand drops out of mine, and her eyes close. I can't say a word as I watch her die, every part of me feeling as cold and distant as the very song she used to sing to me.

"Mum, mum, don't," Alex whines. Everything seems surreal as I feel Dabriel pull me into his arms and whisper what I'm sure are comforting things. All I can hear is Alex's cries and the echo of my mum's last words: *Save us all.*

CHAPTER 10

"What are you doing?" Jaxson asks me as I throw my dagger, and it lands perfectly in the next target. It's been a day since my mum died, and I don't know what I'm doing. Dabriel decided to put off seeing the angels until tonight, and I haven't spoken to any of them. I can't speak about it because it will make it more real. It will make it more heart-breaking that my parents have been killed by my grandfather. That my entire family is dead except for him. Him. The evil son of a bitch that hides in his castle and gets his demons to do his handiwork. Everything he has taken from me just continues to add up, he was destroying my life before I was even born. He was destroying everything before the prophecy was even spoken from my grandmother's lips.

"Do you need me to answer that?" I ask sarcastically, and he glares at me. I ignore him and pick up two more daggers, throwing them into the target and landing them perfectly on either side of the first dagger. I imagine the evil, red eyes as I walk over to the target and pull out the daggers. I see the eyes of everyone who is training in the room on me, but I ignore them. I can't deal with being their queen right now, with being the reasonable one. Death, just more death, and what else will be left in the end if I don't kill him?

"Out, everyone, now," he shouts in the training room, and the twenty or so wolves, witches, and vampires quickly run out the door at Jaxson's growly words.

"You didn't need to do that," I mutter, and he chuckles as I put the daggers down on the bench and turn my back to him.

"Fight me, like we used to," he tells me, and I look over my shoulder, only seconds before he charges at me. I move at the last second, dodging his attack and spin around, running at his back. He turns and blocks my hit, and I slam my leg into his side. He grabs my hip and slams me onto the floor, and I knock his legs out from under him. He slams onto the floor next to me, and I roll onto him, holding his arms down.

"I've always liked you on top," he says as we both breathe heavily, and I lean down, kissing him. Jaxson groans slightly and flips us over as he deepens the kiss, pressing himself into me.

"No sex, we need to talk, lass," he tells me as he breaks away but keeps me trapped under him.

"I don't want to talk," I say, looking to the side, and he grabs my chin, gently pulling my face to look at him.

"I get it. You want to fuck and kill and do anything to forget what happened. We are far more alike than I want to admit, lass. I know you feel guilty, you feel like everyone you love has died, and you have lost that last part of your parents," he says, his tone growing gentler with each word.

"I lost my mum, my sister, and my brother, and I wanted to destroy everything because of that. But I didn't, you know why?"

"Why?" I ask quietly.

"Because I had family left to fight for. You have us, your mates. And Alex who is like a sister to you. You have so much to fight for. We will be at your side, there to make sure we don't lose anyone else," he tells me, and his words crack some kind of barrier I've held onto since my mum died. I burst into tears, and he sits up, pulling me onto his lap.

"You cry now and let it out. Then you are going to hold your head high and walk out that door and be their queen. They are all scared and need their queen to be strong," he whispers to me.

"With you at my side," I whisper.

"I will always be at your side, Winter," he tells me, and gently kisses my forehead.

"**E**verything okay?" Wyatt asks as he walks into my bedroom where I'm putting my belt full of daggers on. Wyatt's blond hair is as long as when we first met, and his jaw is freshly shaven. Somehow, just dressed in smart, black trousers and a white shirt that is slightly undone, he couldn't look more powerful with the massive sword strapped to his hip. He couldn't look more like the vampire king he is meant to be.

"I'm sorry I shut you out, after mum," I say, my voice cracking a little.

"Winter, you can shut me out, throw those

daggers at me, or, in general, just ignore me, and I will still be here for you," he tells me, and I chuckle.

"You would catch the daggers anyway."

"True," he smirks.

"We have angels to go see," I say and walk over, leaning up to kiss him gently.

"I'm proud of you," he tells me, and I nod, letting myself have this moment with him before pulling away. Wyatt takes my hand as he leads us down the corridor. The door at the end opens, and Freddy walks out, followed by a boy I've not seen before. He has wavy, black hair, with what looks like red tips in his fringe. I can't tell what he is, but he seems almost familiar to me. I spend way too long meeting the boy's eyes before pulling my own eyes away.

"Winter," Freddy says when he notices me and runs over.

I hug him, and I'm a little surprised when Wyatt says, "Son, who's your friend?" I know Freddy is his son, yet it's still strange to hear him say that.

"Josh, come here," Lucifer says as he walks down the corridor towards us.

"Is Josh your son?" I ask Lucifer when he places a hand on Josh's shoulder, and Josh looks over at me. The bright blue eyes are so familiar and clash against the tips of red in his hair.

"Yes," he replies tensely.

"So, you're an angel? Sorry, for a second I thought you might be something else," I tell Josh who just crosses his arms and looks at his dad. Josh looks a lot like his dad, I can tell he is going to break some hearts when he's older, much like I can see Freddy doing. The two of them should be locked away from girls.

"Yeah, Dad, why is that?" Josh asks, his voice dripping with sarcasm. Josh and Lucifer seem to share a look before looking back at us again.

"Angels do not get their wings until their sixteenth birthday, and that is why," Lucifer answers, but Josh surprises me by laughing loudly.

"Any kind are welcome here, you don't need to hide anything from us," I tell Lucifer.

"Nah, it's more the issue that my stepmum and half-brothers wouldn't be happy with anyone knowing my secrets, right, Dad?" Josh says.

"Let's go," Lucifer demands, and I watch as they both walk away.

"Your friend is odd."

"He's a half," Freddy tells me, shocking me a little bit, but some part of me knows the truth in his words as I look over at Josh before he walks out of the corridor.

"Half what?" I ask, knowing I was right, and there is something strange about that boy.

"He doesn't know. His dad won't tell him, but he was living with humans until recently," Freddy tells me.

"I'm going to find Mich," Freddy says, reminding me of the deaf wolf that he made friends with. Seems they are still friends.

"Is Mich a half, too?" I ask Freddy, just having a feeling.

"Yes. His dad was a witch, how did you know?"

"A feeling," I say, and Freddy hugs me before walking away.

"Keep an eye on who you make friends with, son," Wyatt tells him, and he turns around at the end of the corridor.

"Careful, you're starting to sound nice, vamp," Freddy laughs before walking away, and I look up at Wyatt who is trying not to laugh as he watches where Freddy was. They are very alike.

"It's weird you have a child, a child that's not mine," I blurt out my thoughts, and then cough, realising what I just said.

"Does it bother you?"

"Sometimes I'm jealous of Demi, that she had your love first. That she had your children first, and then I realise I'm jealous of someone who is dead. I just can't help how I feel," I admit what I've never really said to him. He takes my hand and leads us out onto the balcony, shutting the glass doors behind us. I look over the woods from the balcony, the very place that reminds me of my first date with Atti, and I'm loving the pots of flowers someone has placed out here.

"What I felt for Demi . . . well, I never want to admit it to Freddy, but it wasn't true love. I know that now, but back then, I didn't. It was lust and tiredness of everyone in my home that was so fake towards me. The countless vampires my father tried to make me mate to. The countless humans and vampires I watched him kill. It was just a chance to be happy. I know this because I never felt for her an ounce of what I feel for you. Nothing in my life compares to how I feel for you, you're so much more, Winter," he says gently, his dark eyes willing me to believe him.

"I don't want you to just say that," I whisper.

"I'm not. You will understand one day soon that I love you so much that I would die for you. I would do anything to keep you safe," he tells me and looks away, watching something out in the skies. I know how he feels because I would do the same for him, but more. I would do anything to just have a life with him, with my other mates. I feel like every one of them ran away with my heart the moment we met, and I wouldn't ever chase them for it. It's theirs.

"You won't have to die for me, no one will," I say firmly.

"You mean the prophecy?" he asks, and I nod as he steps in front of me, then I look up at him.

"Someone might die, Winter, and you need to accept that, but it won't be you," he says and tilts my chin with his finger and gently kisses me.

"The last sentence of the prophecy was '*Her saviour will die when the choice is made*'. I don't have an idea who that is, but it can't come true. There has been too much loss," I whisper the end part.

"Then we will make sure that part doesn't come true, but we have an entire race of angels to win over first, My Queen," he tells me and gently kisses my forehead as he pulls me to him. I rest my head on his chest and relax in the safety of his arms, the cold wind blowing around us, but it doesn't matter as everything feels safe in his arms.

"Before the war, I will, and I will announce

Freddy as my heir. He is already heir to the wolf throne, but it will give him extra protection. Is that okay with you?" he asks, and I love him more for asking me. Not that he needs to, I would do anything to keep Freddy safe.

"Yes. I see him as family. I hope one day he sees me like that, too," I reply.

"He already does, Winter. It's how he looks at you, you two were drawn to each other from the very start," he says and lets me go. He walks over and opens the door. I look back at the sun setting over the sky, and the way it sends oranges and reds across the sky. It's so beautiful, like the peace before the storm.

CHAPTER 11

"Remember to stay close, no matter what happens," Atti tells me as I slide my hand into his, and my other hand is held tightly in Dabriel's grip. I can feel the worry through our bond from all my mates. They all don't like this, and I have to admit, I don't either, but we can't leave the angels alone until the council knows everything. Apparently, Lucifer can show the council members if they won't let me show them my memories. The guys decided to all come today with three angels as well as Leigha who demanded to protect me when she heard what we were doing.

"Time to see my home, Winter," Dabriel says gently, and I nod, squeezing his hand and keeping my eyes locked on his as Atti moves us all with his power.

When we get there, the first thing I notice is the loud noise, a ringing noise that makes me want to put my hands on my ears, but both my hands are held in the tight grip of my mates. When I look away from Dabriel, I almost wish I hadn't when I see all the bodies on the ground in front of me and the destroyed building we are standing in. Two demons run at us, not stopping once as they kick the angel's bodies out of the way. Atti lifts his hand, calling his fire and destroying them before they even get close. There are bodies everywhere, of all ages, and sickness fills my mouth.

"Over there," Lucifer says, getting our attention, and we look up to see a bunch of angels in the air, avoiding the arrows the demons on the ground are shooting at them. Most of them are holding children and trying to fly away. This place must have once been beautiful as I look around at the small houses, but all there is now is blood and more death. The demon king didn't send his army here to help them or work with them, he came to kill them all.

"We need to save them, stay here," Dabriel says and lets my hand go, flying over with three angels that came with us. I glance over as Leigha and Wyatt come to my side, and Atti keeps me close as we look around. What once must have been a beautiful building is now just pieces of rock, and I see a painting on the floor under the rubble, only the head of a handsome angel with a white crown can be seen. I take a guess that that was Dabriel's father, the old king.

"We need to help them," I tell Atti, who looks over at the angels fighting and back to me.

"Stay close, I don't think the demon king is here now, but he could come back," Atti tells me. I know the demon king isn't here, this is just a game to him, and he wouldn't waste his time. I doubt he would leave the portal now, knowing that's the only way to keep himself safe.

"I'm going to shift, makes it easier to kill them," Jaxson tells me, and hands his sword to Wyatt before his clothes shred away, and he shifts into his giant black wolf. Jaxson's wolf presses against my side just before we all start walking. I pull one of my daggers out of my belt, holding it at my side and my other hand is in Atti's as we approach the massive group of demons. There are so many angel bodies at their feet, and just behind them are a big group holding off the demons, with what looks like women and children behind them. They are all a mix of white and black wings as they fight, holding each other off.

"I have an idea," I say and step in front of Atti, pulling my power and sending it out like a shock-wave towards the group of demons. My blue wave of power hits them one by one, and they disappear into blue dust. It even pushes some of the demons that escape the wave into the angels. The angels make quick work of killing the remaining demons as Jaxson rushes forward and starts helping them by ripping the demons to shreds with his paws and teeth.

"Your power works against them," Atti whispers.

"I can't do it again, it takes too much," I tell him breathlessly, as I glance over at the twenty or so demons that are still left, but Jaxson is making a good go at killing the demons brave enough to come near us.

"That's what your kings are for," Wyatt says and lifts both his swords, and runs towards the demons. Jaxson runs over at his side and Leigha smirks at me before following them, throwing knifes at the demons that get close. I glance up to see Dabriel fighting with an angel, and I catch a glance at his face, recognising him from the meal.

"What's Dabriel's brother's name?" I ask Atti, who is looking up as well.

"Zadkiel," Atti tells me, just as Dabriel tackles Zadkiel to the ground right in front of us. They both get up quickly, both of them weaponless from the fall.

"You got them all killed, thousands of them must have died because of you. You are their prince, and you betrayed them all. I always knew you were a selfish bastard, but this . . . this is unbelievable even for you!" Dabriel shouts as he holds Zadkiel up by his white shirt and throws him across the field.

"No! Govan did!" Zadkiel shouts back as he stands up, and Dabriel shakes his head, the cuts on his face disappearing.

"Where is Govan? What do you mean?" Dabriel asks, but his tone is so sharp, I doubt that he believes a word his brother says, and I don't blame him.

"Dead. I killed him when he told the demon king where we lived. I never told him that, I just wanted an alliance for my people," Zadkiel says and glances at me. The fear in his eyes when he sees me is clear, and it almost makes me want to attempt to kill him myself. I don't know if his words are true, but he knew the demon king couldn't be trusted. You should never make a deal with the devil. I grew up knowing that, and even most humans wouldn't be stupid enough to make the decisions he did.

"They are not your people, and they will never be."

"You're not going to kill me, brother," Zadkiel laughs.

"I am, and then I'm taking my throne. I'm going to kill you for treason. I'm going to kill you because I don't believe a damn word that comes out of your mouth. I hope the goddess forgives you when you die," Dabriel says, his words echoing around.

"It wasn't me!" Zadkiel protests, his worried eyes glancing between Dabriel and me.

"As a child, you always blamed Govad for your mistakes, and it seems like nothing has changed. You want the throne, then fight me for it!" Dabriel shouts, and calls his marks, which glow on his skin so brightly that I can barely look at him. I glance behind them both to see the battle is over, and Wyatt is walking back to us, unharmed, and throws a sword each to Dabriel and Zadkiel.

"Good luck, my brother," Wyatt says as Dabriel lifts Jaxson's green, metal sword and swings it around his hand a few times. He clearly knows how to use it.

"What is left of the angels is here to witness this fight. Whoever wins takes the throne, and as a member of the council, I decree it," Lucifer says after he flies down and lands next to me. The rest of the hundred, or so, angels stand behind Wyatt, Jaxson, and Leigha on the other side of the fight.

"Don't, you can't interfere. Believe in your mate," Atti whispers when I try to take a step forward as Dabriel smiles at me. He mouths, "I love you," and I do the same. I watch as both Dabriel and Zadkiel bow low and then lift their swords.

"I remember beating you in sword lessons, you never had that skill, Dabriel," Zadkiel taunts and does some complicated show with his sword before dropping into an attack position.

"No, I just refused to kill innocent angels for fighting practise, like you did. Always trying to prove something to someone, Zadkiel. What were you looking for in the demon king?" Dabriel asks, and I watch as Zadkiel's face tightens in anger.

"Do I get your pretty, little, demon bitch to fuck when I become king? Does she come with the throne?" Zadkiel asks, and Dabriel charges at him as I hear Jaxson's wolf growl and feel Atti tighten his grip on my hand. I watch as Dabriel strikes hit after hit on Zadkiel who is only defending from the hits and not getting any of his own in. Dabriel slashes a cut across Zadkiel's leg. I watch as fear fills Zadkiel's eyes, and he tries to fly away, but Dabriel grabs his injured leg and slams him onto the ground. I watch as Dabriel lifts his sword and swings it down on Zadkiel who doesn't move as his head is cut off. The fight is quick, and it wasn't even a fight at all. There was no chance for Zadkiel; Dabriel would never have let him get away with speaking about me like that.

"King Dabriel wins," Lucifer shouts out, and Dabriel stands straighter, throwing his sword on the floor and walking over to me. Dabriel pulls me into a kiss the moment he can, and there's silence as he breaks away from me, linking our hands.

"We have a place that is safe, and we will bring back witches to bring you there. War is coming, and we need angels to help win this. We will never win this apart, now what do you say?"

"May the queen and her kings rule true," a male angel shouts out, and then the rest of the angels repeat the words.

"My Queen," Dabriel says to me gently before he kisses me once more.

CHAPTER 12

"*You are no god,*" *Demtra's cold-sounding voice flitters through my mind as I open my eyes and see my own bedroom, but it's from the past, when it was my grandmother's bedroom. Elissa's body is on the ground where I have a rug now, blood pouring out of her mouth and stomach. I look up to see Demtra and the demon king standing close together, just outside the door. The demon king has some kind of white ward wrapped around his body, so he can't move, and only his head is visible.*

"Does it matter? Your poor little sister is dead, all her mates are dead, and I'm going to find my daughter," the demon king sneers, and Demtra laughs.

"It does matter," she says and lifts the silver circle that opened the portal and drops it on the floor between them. The demon screams as Demtra slams a dagger into her stomach

and falls to the ground, her blood slowly making its way to the silver circle. When the blood touches it, the blue portal opens, spreading and pulling the demon king into it as he screams, but he can't move because of the white ward. There's silence as the blue portal sinks back into the silver circle, and Demtra picks it up. I try to move closer, but as usual, I can't do anything but watch.

"Only one of my blood can open it. Only my blood can close it, it can only be closed with a death," she says, her hand glowing white over the silver ring, and it's clear that her words are a spell of some kind. That they are meant to stop anyone using it to bring the demon king back, but it's too late for that. There's only one person who can die to close it now, and that's me. There isn't anyone else with her blood left.

"No," I shout, watching as she dies, and her lifeless eyes meet mine. I glance between Elissa and Demtra, seeing them both dead and knowing all of the ancestors are dead in this castle too. So much death, and for what? For me to just open the portal and let him back in, it feels like I'm repeating the same mistakes that my family did before me. As the silence of the castle and the death around me hit me, all I want to do is wake up, but I can't. I watch as a girl runs into the room, her brown hair is curly, and I would guess she is a vampire from how pale she is.

"Demtra, Elissa . . ." the woman says, walking slowly into the room with tears falling down her face.

"It's too late, I'm too late," the woman whispers, falling to her knees and taking the silver circle off Demtra.

"Erina," a man with curly, blond hair says as he runs into the room and stops at the sight of the bodies and Erina on her knees. I watch as she closes Demtra's eyes and stands up, holding a hand up to stop the man from walking over to her.

"We have her child, and we will keep her safe, you knew we wouldn't be able to save her, Erina."

"Let's go back to Isa and your mates, it's too late." I hear them talking about my mother, as everything goes black.

"Sleepy head, time to wake up," Dabriel whispers in my ear, and I snuggle myself further into his side. For a moment, I forget everything we have to worry about and just lie with my mate, after a long night of settling angels into the castle. But that doesn't last long as the memories of the war that is coming and the dream haunts my mind. I know it's me that has to die to stop this, there isn't any other way. How am I going to get close enough to the portal and get the demon king through it? I can't use my power like Demtra did and bind him.

"How are we going to survive this?" I whisper, looking up at Dabriel as he leans over me. The morning light casts a light around his body, and his white hair seems almost too bright to look at. He is amazing to look at, I could spend hours looking at him.

"Together. We will make it," he tells me and kisses my forehead. I push him back on the bed and climb over him as I kiss him. He groans when I deepen the kiss, and his hands slide up my back before he shifts us on the bed until I'm underneath him, and I push down his trousers, feeling that he has nothing else on. Dabriel rips my long shirt off me and starts kissing down my neck to my breasts and spends his time running his hands all over me before kissing me again and sliding inside me.

"Dabriel," I moan out when he moves fast, every thrust getting me closer to the edge, and Dabriel shocks me by rolling us until I'm on top. He lets me take control as I lean up, and he runs his hands over me, pushing me closer. When I speed up, and he groans, I know he is close, and he rolls us once more, taking over, and we finish seconds after each other only a few moments later.

"I love you, Winter," Dabriel says gently as we both get our breaths back.

"I love you too, Dab, I always will."

"You sound like you're going somewhere, when there is no chance I'm letting you go," Dabriel says, and I wrap my arms around his chest as he pulls me to his side. He has no idea, I don't want to go, but I know only a death will win this war, and I won't let the past repeat itself. *My mates won't die for me.*

"G ood morning, lass," Jaxson says when I walk out of the bedroom after having a long shower with Dabriel. Dabriel kisses my cheek as he shuts my bedroom door and walks down the surprisingly quiet corridor.

"Morning to you, too," I laugh as Jaxson pulls me close and kisses me.

"You're glowing a little this morning," he says.

"I had a good sleep, Wolfman," I tell him, avoiding saying the wakeup call was better, and he laughs.

"I heard," he says and nods his head towards his own room which is next door to mine. I don't reply, only blush. I don't know why the thought of him hearing me and Dabriel makes me blush, but it does. *Damn, these hot mates of mine.*

"Any more dreams, lass?" Jaxson asks me, thankfully changing the subject.

"No. Nothing unusual," I reply, remembering the dream I had before the demon king took me and what my mum said about Lily, the Fray queen. I need to tell everyone that they might not be helping us at all, and we need to plan for that. I know it was stupid to make that deal, and I was played by that damn fairy. She used my need for a connection to my birth mum to make her seem like a friend to me, when she wasn't. It was smart, but I need to be smarter now. I have four races of people and family I want alive after this war.

"I need to speak to you, and everyone important to the war. I have things about the war I need to tell you all," I tell him, and he briefly frowns but nods.

"Come on then, there's a conference room that we use to talk," Jaxson says and links our fingers as we walk down the corridor. We pass a lot of people, and all of them bow their heads to us as we pass. It used to be weird for me, but I've grown to accept who I am now, I'm not that normal girl who wanted to be a vet. I can't be her anymore, it just isn't in my future. As we pass the different kinds of people, it's strange to see how they have adapted to living together, how they walk past each other like they would pass any normal person in the street. I think every wolf, witch, angel, and vampire here have lost a lot, and that binds people together, any kind of people. Jaxson leads me through the castle and towards the back, which I've not been to before, and we get to a set of three doors. There's a door that leads outside, but Jaxson opens one of the other doors for me, and I walk in.

"I will go and get people, be right back," Jaxson says and leaves me in the massive room. The room has a giant, round table in the middle, made out of a dark wood. There are three large windows that overlook the forest, and there is a big whiteboard on the one wall. I look at the dozens of seats around the table, and the only thought that goes through my mind is the old fairy tale my mum used to tell me about Arthur and the round table. Except this isn't a fairy tale, and my mum isn't here to tell me that story anymore. A loud purr grabs my attention, and I look over to see both Jewels and Mags sitting near the windows. These two used to scare me in their real forms with no glamors to make them look like normal house cats, but now I know they wouldn't hurt me. There's also the fact that there are far scarier things out there than two cats who love shiny things and magazines. I walk over and try not to laugh at Jewels who has one large paw on top of a familiar box. *My crown.*

"Are you keeping it safe for me?" I ask, and Jewels gives me a look that suggests I'm not getting it back. Mags walks over and pushes herself against me, and I stroke her head. Atti loves these two, they are part of him in a way. Or that's what he has tried to explain to me. Not many familiars survived the attacks on the witches' city, or I haven't seen many around the castle. There was a polar bear that I walked past yesterday and tried not jump. Just a random polar bear walking past me, no big deal.

"After everything happens, he will need you." I tell them both, and they seem to understand as they both stare at me. I wonder how intelligent they both are as I look at them, they almost seem sad. I turn and look out the window, watching the breeze move the dozens of different trees in the forest, and the mountains you can see in the background. I don't know how far the trees go on for. They seem to stretch on and on, making them seem endless and beautiful. I look down when I hear some shuffling to see Jewels pick up the box in her large mouth and bring it over to me, dropping the box gently on my feet.

"It's time I wore this, huh?" I ask Jewels, who

tilts her head to the side. I lean down and pick the box up, hearing the door open slightly, and I turn to see Milo fly into the room. Milo lands on top of the box and looks up at me.

"Hey, Milo, you look nice today. Very Robin Hood," I chuckle, seeing the strange, green leather outfit, and he even has a fake bow on his back. I will admit it's likely the cutest thing I've seen, but he has a serious face which is unusual for him.

"Crown keep you safe from blood."

"From blood? Do you mean my demon blood? Safe from the king?" I ask him, and he nods his head with a big smile replacing the frown. I wonder if it's true, but why wouldn't my mum have used it to keep herself safe? I don't have to think of the answer long because I know, but it hurts to even think it. She didn't use the crown because she gave it to my dad, for me. She let herself be taken, to keep me safe. My mum didn't want him to know about the crown because she knew it could keep me safe one day. I lift the lid and stare down at the crown; the large white crystal in the middle and the four crystals encased around it in silver. Red for the vampires, green for the wolves, black for the witches, and the white stone for the angels. I lift the crown, feeling the power spreading through me, and I hear the door open, but I can't look away from the crown as it lightly glows. It's meant for me.

"Winter," I hear someone say, but I close my eyes and place the crown on my head, feeling the power spread through me. When I open my eyes, the room is full of people. Every one of them bows their heads, except my mates who stand strong in a line by the door. They never need to bow to me, they are my equals, as I am theirs. Damn, this crown is so powerful that it floods my mind, making me want to destroy things. I glance down at my hand, seeing it glowing blue slightly and feel for my power, knowing it feels stronger for the extra boost the crown gives me.

"Winter, we don't wear our crowns all the time because they are powerful, meant to be worn in war. They are meant to boost our powers and help us," Atti says gently in my mind, using his gift to appear next to me. I don't move as he takes the crown off me, and the power boost drifts away. I nod at Atti, just as he puts the crown into the box and closes it. Jewels slides between us as everyone comes further into the room and waits for me to say something.

After taking a deep breath, I say, "The crown makes sure the demon king can't control me. I can fight him now, and I can win. My family hid this crown for me, the demon king doesn't know of its existence. It was hidden with my human mother for years and only someone of my blood could open the box. We finally have a way to win, a way to beat him."

The looks of relief around the room are clear. This has been a losing battle until now, we were just hoping for luck to win the war, but this is something else. *This gives us a chance.*

"You can't fight him alone," Atti says gently, looking down at me. I look at him before meeting everyone else's eyes in the room.

"I won't, but this is what I called you here for. Our first meeting of all the supernaturals, the first time we plan anything together. War is coming, and we need a united plan to win. There isn't any other option, so sit or leave," I say, and everyone takes a seat.

CHAPTER 13

"*W*hat was the reason you called us here today, Queen Winter? I have a feeling the revelation about the crown is new to you," Harold asks as everyone finally sits down, and I stand up from my seat. I look around the room at the mixture of supernaturals in here, all of them sitting side by side to plan a fight. Harold, Drake, and Leigha are here for the vampires today. Lucinda, a man I recognise as one of her mates, and Harris are here for the shifters. Then there are three witches, one man and two older women I do not know, but I'm sure they look familiar to me. Representing the angels are Gabriel, Lucifer, and a female angel with long, dark hair and black wings; she also wears a stern expression as she watches me for the answer. I clear my throat before I speak, having the eyes of so many powerful people on me is a little daunting.

"Do any of you know about the Fray? The fairies? Some call them Fey," I ask, and no one says anything until one of the witches I didn't recognise puts her hand up.

"I'm sorry, I do not know your name," I say, and she stands up, bowing before she speaks.

"My name is Duzella. I was on the council for Atticus's mother, and she was a true queen, as well as loyal friend. I was kept in the dungeons until Atticus took the throne, like he always should have. My loyalty is to our king, the rightful heir and the rightful new queen."

"Thank you, Duzella, my mother spoke kindly of you often," Atti says with a sad smile directed at Duzella.

"I've heard stories of the Fray, the ones who live in a dimension next to ours. They say the Fray cross over when the wards between worlds are weak, to cause havoc. There were many books on the Fray in the royal libraries of the witches. Unfortunately, I only read a few, but I will ask around the surviving witches and see if anyone read more than I did. I only saw them as fairy tales, I'm afraid," Duzella tells me.

"Thank you, that would be highly appreciated. Let it be known, the Fray are a very real race, with a very real world," I reply.

"The plants tell me the Fray are not to be trusted, that they only bring sorrow. Their world is connected to ours, with portals only Fray can see. The plants told me about the portals but nothing else," Lucinda tells me. I nod at her and give her a friendly smile. I haven't had time to speak to Lucinda, but I did watch her in training the other day. She was teaching sword skills to some teenagers, they looked terrified of her by the end of the day. Well, except Freddy, Josh and Mich, who loved it. They are all amazing fighters, and it's clear they have been training since they were little, with the way they fought. A clearing of someone's throat makes me come back to the present and remember what I was going to say.

"I apparently can dream-call, a demon power I have. It's a variation of the demon king's power to control his own blood. My mother was rumoured to be able to control people, but I can only control bringing blood relatives into my dreams. I dream-called the Queen of the Fray by accident, her name is Lily, or that's what she told me. But it seems like she played me for a fool by making me believe she was friends with my mother," I say, and Wyatt frowns as I look down at him.

"Just before I was taken and controlled by the demon king, I had a dream. In this dream, my mother, Elissa, and Demtra were there." There's hushed whispers following my words. "They told me about how Lily is no friend of my mother's like I was told, and how she cannot be trusted."

"How does that affect us all, Queen Winter?" Lucinda asks me.

"It's just Winter, no need for the title every time we speak. We have a lot of discussions ahead," I say, and my mates chuckle a little. I hold in the urge to kick one of them under the table.

"I made a promise with the Queen of the Fray. I promised to hand over a half Fray child that is in this world, in exchange for soldiers and weapons on the day of war," I say, and there are more whispers around the room following my words. I wait for someone to say something, knowing that all my mates know of this already, so it's no shock to them. It is a shock that the Fray has tricked me, and the anger written all over each of their faces says it to me. They are as mad as I am.

"It sounds like an easy enough promise, and I don't see how she will get herself out of it," Lucifer says.

"But I disagree, mate. The child part is easy, the offer she made is not. There is always a way around what you promise in a deal. If the Fray are not to be trusted, then we can expect them to betray us," the woman next to Lucifer says.

"I don't trust her. I have no idea if those soldiers will betray us, but I know we need to be prepared if they do," I say, and there's silence around the room for a long time as we think about it. I don't know how she is going to betray me, but I just remember my mother's panicked look when I told her I had made a deal with Lily. She wouldn't have wasted her time warning me otherwise.

"Right, we need a plan, no more waiting around and training," Wyatt says, and there's quiet agreements around the room.

"How are we going to win this war?" Jaxson asks no one specifically, but all of us.

"How many of us are there for starters? Let's talk numbers," Atti asks as he stands up and goes over to the white board. I watch as he gets a marker off the side and opens it.

"We did a head count, and not including

women and children, we have nine thousand and twelve," the vampire who spoke before says, and I feel a sharp pain at the thought of how many have died to get us here. So, so many are lost.

"We have to take into account that it takes at least two of us to kill one. We can get lucky, but we don't have the weapons we know the demon king's army has."

"What is the weapon count? The pack doesn't need weapons, remember that," Jaxson asks, reminding us how the wolves are weapons themselves.

"Neither do witches, not really. Most witches have element powers enough to fight," Atti says. His point is true.

"Okay . . . we have no idea how big his army is, but I'm guessing he has at least ten thousand, if not more, turned humans from Paris alone. We know he has two dragons, and they will be able to fly in," Atti says and writes this on the board.

"Why can they fly in? In the witches' city, the ward had to be broken to let them in."

"I figured this out last night," Atti gives me a worried look, "the wards are always weaker on a solstice. It interferes with them somehow, and I forgot about it. It means the dragons might be able to get through easily."

"Dragon," Milo says, flying off from the window and sitting on the table.

"Dragons. There will be two of them. How do we kill them?" Atti asks Milo.

"Yes, dragon, Milo," Jaxson says.

"I will call dragon," Milo says and flies off towards the door. I shake my head at him, having no idea what he is going on about. We really need to work on making full sentences with him some time.

"We need help, and I doubt the humans will help us with this war, not after Paris," I finally say into the silent room.

"I know a place with supernatural people who may help us because the demons will be after them, too, but a warning, My Queen," Lucifer says, "they might just as easily betray us, this is why I never wanted to tell anyone about them."

"Who?" I ask him.

"My son is half angel, and they came to me once, asking if I wanted to give my son to them to protect. They claimed to have thousands of refugees and halves that are hidden," Lucifer says.

"We cannot trust a load of halflings, my queen

and kings. I've heard of these people, and they will betray you all," Gabriel says.

"Be careful, my son is a half, and I will rip your throat out if you say another word about them," Wyatt snaps, his sentence followed by the wolves' light, warning growls. I place a hand on Wyatt's shoulder.

"We need help, or it doesn't matter whose blood we have. It doesn't matter if we are halves, if we are full bloods, or even human, we will all die the same way. The demon king doesn't care what blood we have, to him we are all dead already, and this is just a game. I suggest we stop acting like children and win the big game," I tell the room of supernaturals, who watch me with fear and hope in their eyes.

"Wise words, My Queen, I am sorry for speaking out of turn," Gabriel says and bows his head.

"Our queen is right. It doesn't matter anymore. We all have family and children we want to keep safe and alive, and we need help to do that," Dabriel says, his sentence hanging around the now silent room.

"Where can we find these people?" Atti asks, leaning over me on the table, his chest brushing against my back. I have to resist the urge to lean back into him with all the eyes of the people in here on us.

"They said you call for them in your mind, they have a witch who listens out for calls about halves. I can get Josh to call for them, and then I will explain," Lucifer says.

"That must be one hell of a powerful witch," Atti comments, and he has a point. I've never seen even Atti use that amount of power.

"The man and woman who came to see me were very powerful. They put a ward around us while we spoke and then just disappeared," Lucifer says.

"Like how witches move?" I ask.

"No. With witches you can see them, a glimmer or something. Supernaturals can always tell when a witch uses their power. This was different, and the people that I saw, I believed were an angel and a vampire, anyway," he says. I can't tell much, but that might be because I never really look.

"Freddy, my nephew, is powerful. Far more than I've ever seen any child," Jaxson says.

"I believe mixing our blood makes us more powerful, stronger," Dabriel comments, and a few people nod. My eyes meet with Leigha's across the room, but she only looks at me for a second before looking at Harris. The look says everything, she wants it to be okay for wolves and vampires to mix. She loves him.

"Call for them, tell them the new kings and queen want to make a deal for help. We want to meet," I tell Lucifer who nods.

"I can't call from here, but I can from the local town. I will go there now with Josh."

"I will take you and protect you," Atti says before I can even offer to send someone to go. I don't like the idea of Lucifer or Josh going outside the castle right now.

"I'm coming, too. Freddy wouldn't forgive me if his new best friend got hurt," Wyatt says, standing up as well.

"I should come," I say, and both Atti and Wyatt shake their heads.

"No, the crowning for Dabriel is in two days and important. I know Alex has a dress she needs you to try on," Atti says, and I groan, looking around for Alex but not seeing her. I dread to know what kind of dress she has planned.

"We will meet the day after the crowning to plan for war. Every person who is going to fight needs to be training. Working together," Atti says firmly and walks out with Lucifer and Wyatt following.

"Soon you will be my Queen, officially," Dabriel says once everyone other than Jaxson has left.

"Erm . . . I want to say I'm looking forward to it, but I don't want to know what dress Alex has planned," I say, and he laughs.

"Dabriel, I need a word," Harris says, poking his head around the door.

"Hey, Harris," I say, and he smiles.

"Hey, Win, but I'm serious, two of your angels are fighting, and it's not good. We have stopped them, but they are talking about the laws of females or something," Harris says with a worried look, and then we hear a loud bang outside the room, followed by the sound of glass smashing.

"Be right back," Dabriel says and kisses me gently before walking out. I look down at Jaxson, who pats his lap, and I move so I'm sitting on him.

"That right there, was a queen I'm extremely proud of," he tells me, and I laugh.

"I thought I was being a little too bossy," I say, hoping I wasn't, but I know they need to get over their silly traditions and hate for halves. Things have to change now.

"It was a major turn on, if you want to know,"

Jax says, leaning closer and trailing his lips down my jaw.

"Oh yeah, I can tell," I say, moving a little on his lap and feeling how hard he is. Jaxson laughs before he picks me up and lays me down on the table, kissing me, pressing his body into mine. Jaxson seems to have as much urgency as me, as we quickly remove all our clothes, and he thrusts into me, capturing my moans with a kiss.

"Best be quiet, lass, we wouldn't want someone to walk in," Jaxson says with a slight growl before he does everything he can to make sure I can't stay quiet.

CHAPTER 14

"What's this?" I ask as I walk into my bedroom after a long day of training and then helping some of the angels move into their new rooms. It's been difficult to move them in, but surprisingly, the witches, wolves, and even the older vampires helped. They seemed to have some kind of change when we turned up with the thousand, or so, angels and told everyone they were moving in.

"Girls night. Everything is so serious, and well, I think we could use a relaxing night in," Alex says as I look around to see her, Katy, and Leigha sitting in front of the fire which is lit. There is a movie on pause on the TV, and I try not to laugh as I see

Milo sat on my bed, a selection of chocolate surrounding him. The little demon looks more than happy, and his green outfit has been exchanged for some duck pajamas. I have no idea where he is getting these clothes.

"And Milo? Milo isn't a girl," I say as I slip my shoes off and walk over, sitting in between Alex and Katy.

"Milo is, well, Milo. He saw the snacks, and here we are," Katy says as she picks up the bowl of popcorn and hands me it.

"I do not blame him one bit," I say, and we all look over at Milo who burps loudly and grins at us all with a chocolate-covered face. We all can't help but laugh, but Milo doesn't notice as he continues eating away.

"The demon is cute, but where does he get the outfits from?" Leigha asks, thinking exactly what I am.

"I don't know," Alex shrugs.

"Milo, come here a sec," I shout over, and he looks between me and the chocolate. I can see it's a difficult choice, but he does get up and fly over. Milo lands on my lap, and I try to wipe some of the chocolate off his clothes.

"We wondered where you got your outfits from," I ask him, and he nods.

"Prime," he says, and I frown at him. *Prime?*

"Oh my God, it makes so much sense now," Alex says, and I look over at her in confusion as she glares at Milo. He looks down, but I see the little smirk.

"Okay, so I have Amazon Prime, and my account kept saying I was buying Build a Bear outfits. Dozens of outfits. Now, I haven't had time to think about it, but . . ." she drifts off as we both look at Milo and start laughing.

"Man delivers to woods," Milo says proudly, and I just don't want to think about the poor person who delivered packages to the woods. Or if Milo actually accepted the package. I can just imagine the poor man's face when a tiny demon with white hair appears out of the woods to sign for the delivery. I bet the man dropped the packages and ran off.

"You even bought a Minions outfit, I mean, what?" Alex says, looking up from her phone.

"Yellow?" Milo asks and then flies off back to my bed and the safety of the food. We all chuckle as we watch him start eating, and Alex mumbles about closing her Amazon account somehow and wondering how he got the password in the first place.

"The demon is lovely, I like him and want to see him in the minion outfit," Katy laughs around a small cake bar she is eating.

"He is, well, compared to the rest of his race," I say.

"Well, come on, you're part demon and pretty lovely, Win," Alex knocks my shoulder, and I drop some popcorn on the floor.

"Look what you did," I laugh and pick a piece up and throw it at her. She only laughs and catches it before eating it.

"Where are all the guys, then?" I ask her.

"Wyatt wanted to talk to them all anyway, so it was easy to convince them to leave us for a night," Alex shrugs.

"So, what are we watching?" I ask.

"It's called *Bad Mom*, it's brilliant," Alex says, and I smirk at her as I glance at her stomach.

"I seriously hope you're not watching this movie for tips?" Leigha says, but there's a small smile as she leans back.

"You're pregnant?" Katy asks in shock, and we all look at her.

"You didn't know?"

"Nope, I missed that memo," Katy laughs, "but congratulations, you'll make an awesome mum."

"Thank you," she says with a smile, sliding her hand into mine and squeezing it before pressing play.

"Shh," I whisper to Leigha as she stands up, and we look down at Alex and Katy who are sleeping on the rug after falling asleep during the film. Milo is sleeping on Katy's stomach, and I gently walk towards the door with Leigha. I get why they are all tired, with the training and the stress at the moment, they aren't the only ones tired these days.

"Can I have a word?" Leigha asks as I open the door for her. I knew she wouldn't want to sleep here when she got up after the movie. She is at training stupidly early in the morning these days. I quietly shut the door behind me, and we walk down the corridor and away from the rooms. We come out of the corridor to the main level, and it's empty. Leigha stops near the bannister to the stairs, and you can see all the way down.

"What's up?" I ask her, and she frowns at me, pushing her long hair over her shoulder.

"He is coming any minute now," she says, and I just lift my hands in the air as a response just as I see Wyatt coming up the stairs with Freddy and a familiar, older vampire.

"Hey," I say as Wyatt gets to me and gently kisses me.

"Winter, you remember Harold?" Wyatt introduces me as Harold and Freddy come over. Freddy hugs me and moves away as I offer a hand out to Harold to shake.

"Queen Winter, it is lovely to see you again and looking so well," Harold says and bows his head as he shakes my hand.

"It's good to see you too, but what's going on here?" I ask, because it's a little suspicious us all meeting in the middle of the night like this.

"We are crowning Wyatt tonight and Freddy as heir, in secret. There is a lot of disruption in the castle, and with our people, I believe it would make more sense to have the crowning private, and we do not have the crown to give Wyatt anyway," Leigha tells me as she walks over.

"What about Jaxson, Atti, and Dabriel?" I turn and ask Wyatt. I do agree with him in a way. The angel crowning is coming up, and there is already enough worry throughout the castle. Wyatt being crowned isn't the issue, it's the fact the vampire crown is on the head of the demon king, and Wyatt is naming a half breed as his heir. There are rules, I'm sure, and it makes everything easier to do in secret.

"They are setting it up," he tells me, but I already guessed he wouldn't keep this from my other mates. They are like brothers to him and, really, the only people we need there.

"Drake?" I ask as Wyatt places his hand on my back, and Freddy takes my other hand as we walk down the stairs.

"There too, but no one else. Leigha, Drake, and Harold are my new council of the vampires and the only ones I need there today."

"Aren't there usually four on the council?"

"Yes, I'm naming Freddy as the fourth."

"You can't do that," Freddy protests, and the statement echoes around the stairs. Leigha glares back at us and places a finger on her lips to suggest we all be quiet.

"I can, and I will. You are the prince of the vampires and heir to the throne. A seat in the council will teach you what you need to rule one day."

"I might not even rule, if Winter has a child, they will be heir to all the races," Freddy says, and Wyatt glances at me with a strange look. He almost looks sad, and it confuses me. *Why would he be sad about the idea of us having a child in the future?*

"No one knows the future, son. For now, will you do this?" he asks. Freddy doesn't say a word as we walk down the final set of stairs. We follow Leigha and Harold down one of the corridors, and they open a door, walking in when Freddy stops.

"I will do this, but it means nothing," Freddy says, not looking us in the eyes as he walks in the room. Wyatt catches my arm as I go to walk in and pulls me to him. I gladly slide my hands around his neck, and he gently kisses me.

"I remembered that I never asked if you want to be my queen?" he says, and I chuckle a little.

"Wyatt, I chose you the moment you kissed me, all the way back then. It's me and you," I tell him, and he nods, resting our heads together for a while as we look into each other eyes.

"I'm lucky to have met you, Winter, to be part of your life," he whispers and then steps away from me as I hear footsteps next to us. I look up to see Jaxson leaning against the door and watching us.

"Are you coming in?" he asks with a smirk, and I roll my eyes at him.

"Coming, Wolfman, so impatient," I reply, making him laugh as Wyatt slides his hand into mine, and we walk into the room. The room is a pretty basic one, with some chairs around, and it's been recently painted, by the smell in here. Harold is standing at the front of the room with Freddy, Leigha, and Drake at his sides. Jaxson joins my mates who are standing near the back of the room, and I smile at them all as Wyatt walks us in. We stop in front of Harold.

"I usually speak the Latin or French version of this, but this time I will use English for the new queen," Harold says gently, and I give him a grateful smile. It would make no sense to me otherwise, and I could be swearing to protect a race of pumpkins and not know it.

"Please bow as I say the ancient words," Harold says, and I copy Wyatt as he kneels and bows his head.

"The council has been chosen, and the chosen have come here to crown their new king and his queen. Royal vampire council crowns the new king.

Only death shall break the vow you will now make. Your souls are now joined and here to protect the vampire race. May the vampires also protect their new king and queen."

"I vow to protect," Wyatt says, and there's silence until someone clears their throat. Crap, I think I'm meant to say that too.

"I vow to protect," I say, and there's silence until I feel a finger under my chin, and I lift my head to see Wyatt standing in front of me.

"This ancient book has the blood of every king and queen that has ruled. You must cut your finger and place your finger on the book," Harold explains, as he comes over with a very old-looking book. *It's a weird thing, but who am I to judge?*

"Okay," I say and watch as Wyatt pulls a dagger out of his suit jacket and cuts his finger quickly. Harold opens the book; one page has two bloody finger prints on it and another language written around the prints. I would guess it's Wyatt's parents' names and their blood. I watch as Wyatt presses his finger on the book and then hands me the dagger. I shake my head and push the dagger into his hand.

"I trust you to do it," I say and hold out my hand for him. Wyatt keeps eye contact with me as he takes my hand, only looking down for a second as he cuts my finger, and I try not to wince at the sharp pain. I quickly place my finger next to where Wyatt had placed his, and Wyatt takes my hand off the book, putting my cut finger into his mouth. I have to admit it's pretty sexy, despite the room full of people watching us.

"Later," I mouth silently as he lets my finger go, and he winks at me in response.

CHAPTER 15

"I seriously doubt you could have chosen a bigger dress, Alex," I say, and she chuckles as she looks at me. The dress has a massive, black skirt at the bottom, with a white frost pattern laced down the dress on one side, and the top part is all white lace. Alex put my hair into a bun that is on one side, and there is a little curled bit left out that shapes my makeup-filled face. I don't usually wear this much, but the smoky eyes and pale lipstick do look pretty. The thoughts of my long night with Wyatt flash through my mind; the things he whispered in my ear as he was inside me. The way he held me in his arms all night afterwards, last night was perfect. Only, when I left Wyatt's room this morning to get dressed in my own, I didn't expect to walk into the selection of dresses and madness that Alex had turned my bedroom into. The dress is every bit perfect for the crowning of the angel king and queen, well Dabriel and me. Alex couldn't have chosen a better dress for me to wear, and even being in it is giving me some confidence about today. The black represents the dark angels and the white lace, the light angels. I want us all to be united, and this dress shows off that. I love that I didn't even have to tell Alex this, she just knew.

"This one isn't as tight as the red one I made you wear last time," she says, reminding me of the night I was stupid enough to let the vampire king use me to open that portal. The dress was amazing, though. I look over at Alex as she straightens her long red hair, and memories of growing up with Alex flash through my mind. I remember the first time I met her and sharing my ice cream. I remember holding her as her parents hadn't fed her in two days and giving her my lunch before taking her back to my house for the first time. Once I told my mum, she adored and looked after Alex as much as I did. Alex was always more of a sister to me, and despite the fact the demon king has killed all my family, I still have Alex. I will fight to the very end to see her live through this war.

"You're my best friend, you know that?" I tell her and walk over, giving her a hug. Alex has on a simple white dress with little black flowers up the sides. *Simple, but stunning.* Her red hair brings that little bit of colour to her outfit, as well as the red jewelled necklace she has on. I don't recognise it, but it's lovely.

"Yes, I think so, although I miss the days where we planned our nights out and not how to survive a war," she replies.

"I miss those, too, but I think this was always planned for us. All of it," I say and place my hand on her still small stomach.

"What did Drake say?" I ask her, and she smiles at me. I haven't had much time to speak to her alone about everyone's reactions to the pregnancy. I know everyone knows but not how she told them.

"He was over the moon and told everyone. I've never seen him this happy," she tells me with a bright, happy smile. Alex is almost glowing recently, with what I'm sure are pregnancy hormones.

"Want to know what the army brat said?" Alex asks me, referring to Leigha.

"Something about locking you somewhere safe, I bet," I reply, knowing what Leigha is like.

"Yep. She insists on training some poor girl to protect me and locking me away," Alex says. *It doesn't surprise me one bit.*

"My mates all say she is amazing at training, that all the people respect and listen to her. Jaxson thinks it's best to let her and Harris work together permanently to train everyone. They are both very good," I say.

"Only because they are scared of her and too scared to say anything about her in case either Harris or Drake hear them. Both of them are seriously protective of Leigha," Alex chuckles, and I remember Leigha training me; I was scared of her, too.

"I think Harris is good for Leigha. He has that playfulness that is good for her. She is too serious on her own," I reply.

"Like how your mates are good for you. Each one of them. I don't know, it's like they make you complete and happy."

"It's because I love them. It's that simple," I say gently, thinking of them as I smooth my dress down, and there's a knock at the bedroom door.

"Come in," I shout.

"It's time," Lucifer says as he walks in. Lucifer has a long black cloak on with dark black clothes on underneath, and there is a clip with double wings holding the cloak together near his neck. His large black wings fold in on themselves, so I can only see the tips of them as he stands waiting for us. He and Gabriel are the only angels left from the council, and it's custom for a council member to walk the new queen to the soon-to-be crowned king. This was explained last night by Dabriel before he left me with Wyatt and went off to play cards and have a few drinks with the other guys.

"Good luck, but you don't need it. You're every bit the queen they need; you're kind, strong, powerful, and most of all, you're meant for this," Alex tells me and walks out as I take a deep breath. She is right, but it's hard to convince myself of it.

"Let's go," I tell Lucifer as I walk over, and he offers his elbow, so I link my arm in his.

"I wouldn't have chosen a better queen for us, even if you are no angel. Only angels have sat on the throne for many years. But times are changing, we as supernaturals are never going to forget this war or the fact it's brought us all together," Lucifer says, and I laugh a little.

"Have I ever told you that the goddess shows me the past in my dreams sometimes?" I ask him.

"No, you have not."

"In the past, all supernaturals lived together in the castle. In peace," I say, knowing that this has worked for the supernaturals in the past, and it will work again. We just need to put our differences aside and work towards our future.

"Can I ask you a favour?" he asks as we walk down the corridor, and he stops us at the top of the stairs. The stairs are lined with flowers, all white, and have been tied to the bannister. Someone has even tied fairy lights around the bannister between the flowers, and the effect is amazingly beautiful.

"You can ask, but I can't guarantee I will be able to help," I reply, knowing as a queen my word is not something I can just hand out to anyone. I've come a long way since I first met everyone, and since then, there is a lot of responsibility resting with me.

"My son Josh is a half and what he is...well, I don't want anyone ever knowing. Especially not him," Lucifer tells me, and I look up at him.

"Why not?" I ask, because I don't believe in anyone not knowing who they are, what they are.

My own past and who I am was kept from me, and that nearly killed a lot of people.

"Because it would destroy him," he tells me, his dark eyes watching me, and I don't know what to say to him.

"Did you love his mother?" I finally ask.

"No, my sister loved his father," he tells me, and it starts to make some sense now. I know angels only mate to one person, so having a child with another would have to have happened after he was mated. I know this does happen because of what Dabriel told me of his father and his siblings.

"So, he isn't yours?" I ask gently.

"No, but no one can ever know that. My mate, well, she dislikes Josh but won't ever tell the secret of where he came from. She was bound by my sister before my sister died in childbirth. Angel births are difficult to survive, and with who his father is..." his sentence drifts off when some witches in cloaks walk past us, stopping to bow to me before going down the stairs.

"What is it you wish from me?" I ask him gently when they are gone, understanding that this is big for him to tell me. I have the feeling he never told anyone other than his mate this.

"If I die in this war, protect him as your own.

Tell him that his parents are both alive but in a place no one can return from. That they could only be together that way."

"But you said his mother died?"

"She did," he tells me, and I just don't understand what he is saying. If she is dead, how is she with her partner?

"That doesn't make sense," I say.

"I can't, I can't tell you anymore..." he says firmly, but the slight quiver in his tone suggests he wants to tell me more.

"You're blood bound," I say, realising straight away why he can't tell me. This must have been what it was like for Jaxson not to say anything about Freddy.

"I will protect him, if I can," I tell Lucifer, who takes a deep breath at my words.

"And I will protect you on the battlefield and your mates, My Queen," he says and nods his head at me before starting to walk us down the stairs.

When we get to the bottom, there is a mixture of people standing around, all in white or black with their heads bowed. Some are in cloaks, and some are in wolf form. The very presence of all these supernaturals, standing together to crown the angel king and queen, is amazing. We walk down

the pathway in the middle of them, which is sprin-
kled with white rose petals on the floor, as I look
around the entrance hall. We eventually get outside,
where I see my mates all standing together, one
after the other, next to an archway of white and
black roses. My eyes run over all of them. Wyatt,
Jaxson, and Atti have black shirts and black trousers
on, with white roses pinned on the pockets. Dab has
a white shirt and black trousers, with a black rose
pinned on him. They all look extremely handsome
as they stand there, and all I can think of is how
good they look without their clothes, too. After
getting my hormones in check, we walk down the
pathway, and Lucifer lets go of my arm, handing it
to Dabriel.

Dabriel pulls me close to him, whispering as he
brushes his lips against my ear, "You look so beautiful, Winter."

I blush, and he smiles as he pulls away from me
to face the old angel standing under the arch. I walk
forward with Dabriel, remembering this angel is
called Gabriel and the last light angel on the council
to survive the battle. I haven't spoken to him much,
just a little with Dabriel, but he comes across as
firm. The angel has long grey hair, which I'm sure
was white when he was younger, and large wings

much like Dabriel's. His light purple eyes watch me, and he smiles as he starts to speak.

"Thank you to everyone that came here today to witness the crowning of the King of the Angels and his Queen. I never expected to crown a king like this, with not only angels, but witches, wolves, and vampires to watch. I feel this is how we will survive from now on, united together against a war that threatens us all. We need our royals to win this, for it's what the prophecy told us, and the only way I feel we will win," he says, and cheers follow his words through the crowd. Gabriel walks over and picks the crown out of a box that a male angel holds behind the arch before walking back over. Dabriel lets go of my hand to kneel down and lower his head.

"I crown King Dabriel, King of the Angels."

The cheers that follow Dabriel being crowned are so loud I'm sure the world can hear them, and they seem to go on for a long time as Dabriel stands up, his purple eyes glowing. The crown is just as powerful as the others, with white, almost silver stones inside the silver swirls. I pull my gaze away when Dabriel links our hands and holds them up in the air.

"Queen Winter!" Dabriel shouts, and then

everyone shouts my name back, the sound filling the outside. The angel ceremony is far simpler than the vampire one, the crown seems to be important to them. I look over to see Jaxson and Atti with their crowns on, and the absence of Wyatt's crown is noticeable. I don't feel you need a crown to rule, you can rule on your own.

"We will win this," Dabriel whispers as he lowers our hands and slides his other hand onto the back of my head, kissing me. I hope he will win this too, and that the price isn't too high to do so.

CHAPTER 16

"I should come," I hear Freddy say, a slight growl slipping in with the words. I walk around the corner, and see Freddy arguing with both Jaxson and Wyatt. I have to admire Freddy, he is standing up to both of them, holding his ground. There aren't a lot of people who would do that at his age, but also, he is going to be a handful when he is older.

"It's not safe for you," Wyatt responds firmly, his hands on his hips as he stares down his son.

"It's not safe for Winter, but she gets to go. You need me there; I'm a half, and they might actually talk to you if they know you look after me and don't care," Freddy points out, making a valid point. I don't want to take him with us. It will be dangerous, but I know we could easily protect him with all of us there. Not to mention, he can look after himself, too. We need to convince these people, we will need them in order to save everyone and stand a chance.

"He has a point," I say, walking over, and they both look down at me. I hate being short sometimes, next to all these tall guys. Freddy is even growing and is now about my height.

"Not happening, lass," Jaxson says, shaking his head. *Stubborn wolf.*

"I will protect him, so will you and Wyatt. Atti and two other witches are coming as well," I point out. It only takes seconds for any of the three witches coming to bounce Freddy out of there.

"I'm not using my nephew as bait," Jaxson says, shaking his head at me.

"I wouldn't ever do that, Jaxson," I snap back, and his face drops.

"Sorry. I just can't lose him, not after everything, and my wolf doesn't like it," Jaxson says. I walk over to him and rest my head on his shoulder. I get it, everything is beyond stressful at the moment.

"I'm suggesting that I've seen Freddy fight, and all of you are very powerful. There is no way we would let anything happen to him, but we need these halves to talk to us. Freddy may be the best chance. No offense, but all of you guys are scary and intimidating. Bringing Freddy may just help us," I tell him, and he looks at Freddy, who has a long sword strapped to his back and the same determination on his face that his dad and uncle always have. I don't want to take him, but I don't think we have much of a choice. The war is five days away, only five. Every time I go to sleep, I beg for a dream, or for my family to come to me, but it's not working. I haven't spoken to Elissa or my mum since the dream before I was taken. I need to talk to them because I know the prophecy is coming true, and the price is my life. I need to be certain it's me that is paying this price. I feel, more than ever, like I'm missing something.

"Fine, but you stay by a witch and my side the whole time," Wyatt says, with Jaxson nodding in agreement.

"Awesome," Freddy says with a big grin aimed at me, before running over to Atti and the two witches chatting by the door.

"You ready for this?" Wyatt asks as he comes closer and holds my hand. I look over at him, seeing the vampire I love, but he looks beyond hot today with his sword on his back and the suit he has on.

"To try and convince a load of people that have hidden from us, for years, to fight for me? Yeah, sure. It's just like convincing Alex that salad is a real food," I say, making him and Jaxson laugh. I've never actually seen Alex eat a salad, she doesn't need to, apparently. I know if I didn't force myself to eat a salad at times, I would be huge.

"I heard you're going to be an auntie," Wyatt says gently.

"So are you, you know Drake sees you as a brother," I remind him.

"Maybe," Wyatt says, but a flash of pain flies over his face. It's gone quickly when he blanks his expression. I go to ask him what happened there when Atti distracts me.

"Time to leave," Atti says as he walks over and wraps his arms around my waist, kissing my cheek. I laugh as I feel him use his power and move us. When we reappear, it's at an old building in the middle of a forest I've never been to. Atti lets me go slightly when Jaxson and Wyatt appear with one witch and Freddy with another. The witches have their hoods up, so I don't know who they are.

"Why here?" I ask again as I look around. Atti said the halves never came to meet them when Josh called them. They placed a message asking to meet and an address in their minds. It really bothered Atti because he couldn't see where they were. I think he is just curious about how powerful these halves are.

"It was part of their agreement. We couldn't exactly say no, as it would be a sign that we don't trust them," Atti tells me, and I agree. He has a point, but I still don't like where they have chosen to meet us. I jump when a ward appears around us and the house. It's white and large enough to spread up to the trees, but I can't see who is making it. My mates move closer to me, just before the door to the house is opened.

"You are right not to trust strangers, witch King," a voice says, and I watch as three people come out from inside the house. One is an angel, with dyed-blonde hair and large, black wings. She has on a mini black top and worn jeans, showing off her stomach. She is extremely beautiful, but the slightly cruel smirk on her lips suggests I shouldn't trust her. The other two are sisters, I would guess, with brown hair and matching blue eyes. Atti told us that someone called Mila and Soobeen would be meeting us, they told them the names in the brief conversation they had. I couldn't tell the twins apart, not as I look between them. They both have worn tops on, and leggings underneath. The main thing I can see is how thin they are. It's not a natural thinness either, their cheeks are too hollow, and I have a feeling they aren't well.

"I'm guessing one of you is Soobeen and the other Mila?" Jaxson asks, stepping closer to Freddy when all three of them ignore us to stare at him. Freddy holds his head high, meeting each one of their gazes and doesn't show any fear. It's really good to see him so strong with everything that is planned for us.

"The rumours are true, sister, they really do have a half in the royal family," one of the sisters says, and the other one nods. It's extremely difficult to tell them apart at this point.

"I'm Soobeen, and this is my sister Mila. This is Chesca," Soobeen introduces her, and her eyes lock with mine for a moment before she looks back at Freddy. I glance at the angel called Chesca, who gives me a small smirk as she tilts her head to the side and then looks at my mates. When she winks at Jaxson, my power automatically comes out, and I step forward without realising I've done so.

"Please ignore Chesca, she is half succubus demon, and flirting is in her blood. She won't touch your mates, Queen Winter," Mila tells me firmly, a worried look crossing her face. It doesn't surprise me that the angel is a demon of some sorts.

"Winter, it's okay," Atti whispers and puts an arm around my waist as I try to calm my powers and myself down. All I can think about is ripping the angel's wings out for flirting with my mate.

"Behave," Soobeen tells Chesca who sighs but looks away from us all to look at her nails.

"I will speak to the Queen and the half boy, alone," Soobeen says, and Jaxson's growl is all that needs to be said on the matter.

"Give us a minute," I say loudly, and Soobeen nods at me, understanding that I need to talk to them about this. We all walk back off into the woods a little, close to the ward.

Jaxson says, "There is no fucking way I'm letting you and Freddy go in there alone."

"We don't have much choice. I don't want to, but I'm not weak, and I saw the fear in their eyes when my powers came out. I don't think we are a threat to them. Look at how they are dressed, how thin they all are. I think they need our help as much as we need theirs."

"I will protect her, too," Freddy says and comes to stand next to my side.

"They have fifteen minutes, and then I'm

coming to get you." Atti pulls me closer to him, kissing my cheek. "Until then, I can speak in your mind," Atti whispers the end part just for me.

"I don't like it," Jaxson says.

"Neither do I, but I trust Winter and Freddy. I've seen them both fight and know they can do this," Wyatt says, and I see Freddy give him a strange look. It almost looks respectful.

"At the end of the day, if they kill me, the demon king wins, and they will never be safe because you would all kill them. The demon king doesn't want me dead, so even if they are working for him, they won't kill me. I will shout in my mind for you if I sense the demon king, but I don't think he is stupid enough to fight you all out in the open like this," I say, knowing it's true.

"I would love to fight the bastard," Atti says.

"That's the point, he won't fight you alone. He is a coward that hides behind his army. If he wanted to fight you, he could have done so easily in the castle, but he didn't, he came for me when I was alone," I say, and Jaxson pulls me into a hug when I step away from Atti.

"Fifteen minutes," he says and kisses me gently. Wyatt and Atti nod at me as I hold Freddy's hand and walk over to the sisters and Chesca. The closer

I get to them, the more I feel like I can trust them for some reason. I don't get why it is, and it's not something I can explain to my mates. *There's just something.*

"You have fifteen minutes," I tell them, and Mila nods at me in response. They all look between each other for a second, but I see it.

"Sure," she says and walks into the old ruined house. The house looks like it could be blown away any minute, and the inside isn't any better. There is nothing inside, other than a burnt-out fireplace and a massive, red rug that's covered in dirt and burnt in places. It stinks of smoke in here, making me wonder if there was a fire recently. I watch as Soobeen pushes the old rug across the floor, and Mila opens a hidden door in the floor. The loud creaking of the door is the only sound, and it's eerily quiet.

"This place looks like the Shrieking Shack," Freddy whispers.

"It does," I whisper back, wondering why the place looked familiar to me.

"This isn't a book about witches, little boy," Chesca snaps before walking down the steps in the trap door.

"I know," Freddy says but smirks at me. I try not to laugh at his attitude.

"Come," Mila says and walks down the steps, with Soobeen holding the door open. I walk in first, making Freddy walk behind me, and take the steps down to the dark room below. The steps are lit up by small fires in sconces on the walls, and the steps are pure stone. There isn't anything to hold on to as I take each deep step, and it takes everything in me not to trip up. I could just imagine tripping over and crashing into Chesca in front of me. I doubt she would take it well.

"Everything okay?" Atti asks in my mind, almost making me jump and fall down the steps like I was thinking about.

"Dammit," I mutter out loud.

"Be careful, Queen Winter. The steps are difficult down here until you know how to walk down," I hear Chesca say, and the sarcasm in her voice is overwhelming.

"So far, so good," I think, but know he can't hear me, and I feel a little stupid until I remember he actually asked me a question, so it's natural to answer.

"I can hear you when you project your thoughts like that,

it's a witch mating thing," Atti says, with almost a laugh.

"Then we are walking down a creepy, underground staircase, and I'm trying not to pull the annoying angel's hair out," I tell him, and I can hear his laughter in my head for a little while as I concentrate on walking down. I feel Freddy place his hand on my back a few times, the steps are just as large for him to walk down, and it's comforting to know he is okay despite me not really being able to see him.

"Be careful," I hear Atti say, his tone gentle.

"Love you," I say back, and then there is silence, but I know he heard me, and that's enough. I bet he is telling the others about what I said. I look forward as we get to the end of the stairs from hell, and there is a clear ward. I can't see anything through the ward, despite it being clear.

"You must walk through the ward. It will not interfere with your bond and your mate hearing you," Soobeen says behind me, and I can't see her in the dark, but I feel Freddy place his hand into mine.

"If this is a trap, I will destroy you and everything else," I warn her, before turning and walking through the ward, pulling Freddy with me. When we get through, it's nothing like I would have expected. The ward is hiding a whole town under-ground, with lights strung across the ceiling and dozens of tents on the ground. Various people stop to stare at us and me at them. They are very different, and I can tell from one glance around that they are mainly halves here. Some angels have white and black mixed wings, some witches' hair is mixed, too. One teenage boy stops and stares at us. His black hair has bright blue tips that match his blue eyes. The boy looks at Freddy for a long time before smirking and running off.

"This is no trap, we want something as well, and we need to show you our life. The ward is blessed, it will only let those who mean us no direct harm through," Soobeen says as she stops next to me, and the silence of all the people who stare at us seems to carry her words. The underground cave is amazing to look at, it is really something. I love how the lights are hung on the roof of the cave, and in the walls, there are carved steps and little caves. The only things that concern me are the tents and the amount of people that must live down here. There is no sunlight, no running water that I can see, and no plants. It isn't a great way for anyone to live.

"Then, show me," I respond, smiling kindly at her.

"We will be fine from here," Soobeen tells her sister and Chesca, who bow to us before walking away. These three must be the current leaders of the halves. People start to move away from us when they leave, and noise seems to return to how it was before we came here.

"For too many years, we have hidden underground and away from both humans and supernaturals," she tells me. "Please, let us walk as we talk," Soobeen requests, and I nod, putting my hand on Freddy's back to lead him away from whatever he is staring at.

"Why hide from humans?" I ask her as she walks next to me. We make our way to a long path in the middle of the tents and some little make shift shops, by the looks of them. I pass a group of children playing. The children can't be older than seven, and they are running around a stick in the ground. Their laughter is sweet, even to my ears.

"The humans are just as bad as supernaturals. We do have some humans here, with their half children. But then, we have a lot of half humans whose parents didn't want an unnatural child."

"'Unnatural' is not a word I would use to describe anyone half human," I say, feeling defensive because I was half human and lucky enough that my mum didn't care.

"Yes, I agree. You say this because of who you are, but then everyone knows your story, Queen Winter. You were fortunate not to have powers as a child, no outward appearances that gave you away. Most of our people are not so lucky, and 'unnatural' is a word we hear far too often," she tells me, just as a man walks past, and I almost stop walking. The man has his mark on his face, the vines of a flower all over his forehead, and also, he has fur on his arms. I don't know what he is, but he nods at us both before walking on.

"I understand," I tell Soobeen.

"Safe still?" Atti asks in my head.

"Yes, and you won't believe what is down here," I reply and follow Soobeen as she gets to a large tent. She slides inside through a flap, and I hold it open for Freddy before following myself.

"Please sit," Soobeen offers and waves a hand at three old-looking chairs seated near a fire. There isn't much in the room to look at, not that I expected much. The bed looks years old, and the furniture is the same.

"You know what we want, what we need," I start to say, and Soobeen holds a hand up.

"You should know your grandfather came to us, only a day ago," she tells me, and my blood runs cold as I stand up off the seat. Freddy pulls his sword out and moves closer to me.

"I don't see him here, now, and that's lucky for you," I respond, and she laughs.

"I wouldn't bring you here if that were so. Now, boy, put the sword away, and both of you should sit down," she suggests, and I place my hand on Freddy's arm.

"It's okay," I say, sitting first, and Freddy keeps eye contact with Soobeen as he puts his sword away and sits down.

"He gave us two days to make a decision, fight with him or die. He could walk through our wards like they didn't exist, and I don't believe it was because he wished us no harm. The army of demons he brought with him told me he was never here to discuss peace."

"Not much of a decision. Knowing the demon king, he will kill you anyway. The same deal was made with two of the angel princes, now both of them are dead and thousands of their people," I respond, and she nods. She must have known about what happened to the angels.

"We have three thousand men and women, who

are strong and can fight. Mixing our blood makes some of our abilities extremely strong," she tells me.

"How many children and people that cannot fight do you have?" I ask her.

"Five hundred," she responds, and I nod. I look around the tent that has holes in it, the fire that is made from old wood and little else. They don't have much, but they have been on the run so long.

"I have a suggestion," Soobeen says, and I nod, wanting to hear it.

"You will have our support, our alliance, and we will fight on your side. I will bow to you as Queen, and all your mates as our Kings." She tells me just what I wanted her to say. This is what we need.

"But?" I ask, knowing that every deal comes with a price, and she smiles.

"You make a law, a law that bans any aggression against halves. A law that recognises halves as a breed, and we become part of the council for supernaturals."

"How do you know about the council?"

"We know many things here. We know you have three representatives from each race. We want three on your council, it would be me, Chesca, and Mila," she tells me.

"Why don't you take your people and run? Let

us deal with the war. You haven't come to us before this, and I'm confused why you have invited us now," I ask, because they have been hiding throughout the supernatural wars that have already happened.

"We don't want to live like this, I don't want my people to live underground and hidden for the rest of their lives because of who they are," she tells me.

"Freddy is a half, and heir to both the shifter and vampire throne. Freddy is on the wolf council and will be attending meetings when he turns sixteen. He will also be heir to the angel and witches, unless I have a child, but then that child would be a half, anyway. I will never let the mere fact that he is a half be used against him. Things are changing already, and I feel I would be offering you little in return for your army and help. This is already going to happen, halves will be accepted," I say firmly. I don't want to make a deal with her for something that is going to happen anyway. That's lying to her and not how I want to be. I'm not a queen built on lies.

"You are a smart Queen and said the words I needed to hear," Soobeen says, leaning forward and tilting her head at me.

"That was a test?" I ask with a small smile. It's a smart move on her end, too.

"Yes. If there was any way you wouldn't accept your own stepson, then there is no way I could trust you," she tells me. I look over at Freddy, who grins. I've never heard anyone refer to him as my stepson, but I do like him being called it. I would be proud to be any kind of mum to Freddy.

"So...we have a deal?"

"You still want a deal for those things, despite the fact that most would happen anyway?" I ask, and she nods, holding her hand out for me.

"Winter, it's been fifteen minutes, do you need us?" Atti says.

"No. We are making a deal now, and they can help us. I'm fine," I say back and feel relief down my bond with them all only a minute later. I lean forward and shake her hand.

"I will give you the places on the council and a safe home in the castle for your people. There are a lot of us living there now, but there are many houses in the woods, so we will find room," I tell her, and she looks relieved as she lets go of my hand and sits back.

"Thank you, My Queen. I will move our people

to your castle tonight, I hear it's the only place safe now?" she asks me.

"Until the Winter solstice. That is when the war is coming. I will be honest with you, the demon king will send his army to destroy us. It's going to be one hell of a fight," I tell her, and she nods, standing up.

"Our people have lost a lot, but there is finally hope with you on the throne. A half human, quarter demon, and quarter goddess. Any child you may have would be more than a half could ever be. You are our hope."

"I have one more question before we leave," I ask, not standing up with her.

"Yes?" she asks me, sitting down once more when she sees the serious look I'm giving her. I know there's a chance the royal half Fray child is here, and I can't be anywhere near the child. I need to make sure that part of my promise never comes true.

"Are there any half Fray children here?" I ask.

"You know about Fray?" she asks me, and I nod.

"One boy," she tells me, with a nervous expression.

"I need to meet him," I tell her.

"Why?" she says, and I can't miss the hostility in her tone this time. The boy must be close to her.

"I made a promise with the Queen of Fray for her help in the war. I know I've made a mistake, but I promised to send a half Fray child over to her, a royal that she said she cannot find here on earth." I tell her the whole truth, there is no point clouding the truth when it's clear the half Fray boy means something to her.

"My son is the only half Fray here, and he is no royal as his father told me he was a guard, but you may meet him to make sure," she says. "I will call my sister to bring him here," she tells me, before her eyes glow white, and she is silent for a little while. When her eyes return to normal, I wait a little before saying anything.

"What do you know about the Fray?" I ask her, knowing that she might be able to tell us something about the help they will bring.

"I met my son's father only once, and it was a one-night stand. I don't know much about their kind, but my son has control over storms and water. I'm a vampire mixed with an angel, so that is not from me, and no, I didn't get wings when I received my powers. The Fray I met had dark blue hair and strange, blue flower-like marks down his arms. My son doesn't have those marks yet, but he is only fourteen," she tells me, knowing that most supernaturals don't get their marks until they turn sixteen. They also get their extra powers. I glance at Freddy, wondering what he will get then, if any. He is already so strong, with his immunity to silver and fast healing.

"Thank you for telling me that," I tell her, and she nods.

"I was young and foolish, he was gone before I even woke up the next day. I remember him saying something about it being the summer solstice," she tells me. It makes sense that the Fray had come through the wards then.

"Did he tell you what he was?" I ask her.

"I have a gift, I can tell what someone is from simply looking at them. When I walked into the night club, I saw him straight away. I had never seen a Fray before, and he told me that he came from the Winter court of the Fray," she tells me.

"Winter court?" Freddy asks, curious like I am.

"Yes, he told me there are four courts, but not much else." I wonder if they are all seasonal. Like Winter, Autumn, Spring and Summer courts.

"Anything you can think of, I would appreciate the knowledge," I tell her. I feel like I should never have made that promise to Lily when I'm clearly blind to their world and everything in it. I shouldn't have, I should have just woken up and tried to deal with this fight on my own.

"I will send someone to bring your mates and witches in here," she tells me, and I nod at her, watching as her eyes turn that white again.

"Atti, they are sending someone to bring you all in here, we have a deal," I shout out in my mind for him to hear.

"What did you offer them?" Atti asks me.

"Nothing that I wouldn't have given them freely," I say back.

Atti chuckles in my mind as he speaks. *"That sounds like I need more of a description in a while. I love you, Winter."*

I look over to see the flap of the tent being opened and a teenage boy coming in. It's the same boy I saw when I first passed through the ward, his blue tipped hair is easy to remember. It matches his unusual, bright blue eyes.

"Nathaniel, this is Queen Winter and her stepson, Freddy," Soobeen says standing up and walking over to the boy who watches us all. I wouldn't say he is nervous, but there is something there. I don't feel any old magic or anything as I walk over and offer the boy my hand to shake.

"Just Winter, no need for all that," I say, and he smiles.

"You don't look like a queen," he points out straight away, and I look down at my leather outfit and daggers on my waist.

"Nathaniel, that was rude," his mum scolds, and Freddy laughs as he comes over.

"You're right, I look like I'm some kind of assassin or something," I say, and he chuckles.

"I'm Freddy," Freddy introduces himself as he steps next to us.

"Nice sword," Nathaniel says, and Freddy pulls it off his back.

"Here," he hands the sword over, and they start speaking. I walk off with Soobeen as we both watch them and wait for my mates to come here.

"They say halves are drawn to each other, much like all supernaturals feel more comfortable around their own kind," she tells me, and I completely agree with her as I watch them talk.

"It makes some sense if you really think about it, nature's way of getting people to stay close to who they are like," I say.

"Are you and Freddy close?" she asks me.

"I like to think we are, I would do anything for that boy," I say, thinking of how we first met and how protective I was over him at the start. There was always something that drew me to protecting him far more than I should have really. I've always liked kids, but with Freddy it was an instant bond. A need to look after him.

"It's because you're a half like him, and there is always that draw to each other," she tells me.

"Like how I feel safe here?" I ask, because it's true. I've felt a sense of safety from the moment I passed through that ward and felt no threat from these people.

"Yes, in a way. I want to be completely honest with you," she says, turning to look at me.

"Okay?" I ask her.

"Some of the people we have here are exiled from the supernaturals. Some for crimes, others have done things in their pasts and are known by everyone at the castle, but have changed as they live here," she says.

"They get one chance, that's it. Make it known that I won't have anyone betray me. I get that not all of your people will want to live in the castle permanently, but here is the deal: if they fight for us, then they are free to leave, and we won't punish them for their past. That deal has no reflection on anything they do after war, though," I say, and she bows her head at me before looking up once more.

"A fair deal," she replies. I look over at Freddy and Nathaniel, the future we are fighting for is always going to come with repercussions, but it is worth it. We have to make sure everything here is worth it.

CHAPTER 17

I swing my fist down on Leigha's arm as she slides to the left of me, and I jump over her leg that she aims at my feet. She jumps away when I catch her, but I don't pause as I follow her, swinging my own leg at her stomach and sending her flying across the training room.

"Fuck, princess...you beat me," Leigha says as I offer her a hand up.

"Never thought you'd see the day?" I ask as I laugh a little and get my breath back. This is what training day and night for the past two weeks has done to me. I was close to beating her before, but I needed to do this.

"No, I knew it was in there, just needed a little push," she chuckles.

"Yeah, there is pushing, and then there's whipping my ass since we met," I laugh out.

"Hey, I still let you eat chocolate," she tells me.

"Only because I would have attempted to kill you if you stopped me," I laugh, but it dies off as I look around the training room. There are so many of us training in here, and I spot Jaxson just as his wolf lands on another wolf. He lets the other wolf go and shifts back, completely naked and explains what the other wolf did wrong. I let my eyes run down his back, and his wolf mark on it.

"Wolves have literally no worries about nudity, do they?" Leigha asks, and I laugh.

"Not one little bit, but you should know that, you know with Harris," I say, and she whacks my arm.

"We actually spend time, not naked, together," she says with red cheeks.

"You love him?" I ask her, and she nods.

"I'm worried about losing him. The war is two days away," she says, reminding me what I already know. It only took us a day to move in the halves and everyone else, but the amount of fights my mates and everyone had to break up was crazy. The people seemed to forget about winning the war to make enemies with the new race that moved in. It took a lot of work and arguments in council meetings to get everyone on board with the new plan. The other council members had mixed views on bringing halves into the meeting and giving them their rightful places, but no one had the guts to say anything after Jaxson punched one of them. They shouldn't have said anything rude about halves in the first place, so I didn't exactly disagree with Jaxson.

"I can't tell you that you won't lose him, but make the most of the time we have, while things aren't certain," I tell her gently, knowing that's all I want to do. I want to spend time with my mates and the people I care about, but here I am in training.

"You should take your own advice, too," Leigha says and nods towards Dabriel and Atti who are speaking to each other by the doors to the training room.

"Later, army brat," I say, and she laughs as I walk off. Dabriel and Atti stop talking when I get close, and Atti pulls me into his side, kissing the top of my head.

"How's training going?" he asks.

"I beat her, can you believe it? I don't think I've ever been as happy to knock her on her ass," I say, and Atti laughs.

"That angel is crazy," I point out, watching as Chesca picks up two knives off the side and then throws them in the air, catching them perfectly. Unfortunately, she is wearing even less clothing than the first time I saw her. Now, there are just tight mini shorts and an even smaller black top.

"She kills the people she sleeps with, so no matter what she looks like, she is evil."

"Chesca does what to her lovers?" I ask, because I'm sure I didn't hear him right.

"She kills them," Dabriel says.

"Why?" I ask as I look over at the dark angel with dyed-blonde hair. She is very beautiful, and a few guys are staring at her, you can't blame them.

"I've heard it's because she gets jealous," Dabriel shrugs, and Chesca chooses that moment to look over at me. She winks.

"How do you know that about her?" I ask Dabriel.

"She was exiled from the angels after her trial five years ago. I remember it well because she was a half. The angels kept her as a baby, and the council raised her, not knowing for sure what she was but that her mother was angel. She killed two of her lovers, both angels and then tried to run away with her newborn son. The child was taken off her, and she killed another angel trying to get to the child, before she was forced to leave."

"Why would they take the child off her?" Atti asks.

"She couldn't be trusted with a child after her killing spree. The council said they had proof she had killed more than just the two we knew about. Her only excuse in the trial was that those men had used her for sex, and she didn't want them to be with anyone else," Dabriel answers.

"And the child? Is he here?" I ask.

"No idea," Dabriel answers with a sad look. We both know how many angels died in the attack, so she could have very well lost her child. I watch as Chesca walks away into the castle and then look around at the army of training soldiers.

"How is the training going? How are the halves doing today?" I ask, wanting to change the subject.

"Training is going as well as can be expected at this point," Dabriel answers.

"The halves are something to be admired. Their power is amazing, and I feel more confident than ever about winning the war," Atti says, and nods his head over to the left. I follow his direction to see a man sitting on the ground with his hands in the dirt. All around him, three small trees are growing slowly from the ground.

"Good, but I'm going back to my room, want to join?" I ask. I would try to make my tone more seductive, but I know I'd end up just sounding weird. I also don't know which one of them I'm even asking. I know they both won't come with me, but I just want to be alone with them.

"Let's all go," Atti says, shocking me when Dabriel nods, placing his hand on Atti's shoulder, and Atti uses his power to move us. I'm not surprised when I see it's my bedroom, they don't seem to use their own very often.

"Let us," Atti says, leaning down and kissing me. I never thought much of the idea of being with more than one of them at a time, but as I feel Dabriel step behind me and start kissing the side of my neck, it doesn't seem like a bad idea. Dabriel rips my shirt and training bra off, the ripped material falling to the floor as his hands slide between me and Atti to roll his finger around my nipples. I moan and break away from Atti's kissing to lay my head back on Dabriel's shoulder. Atti kisses down my chest and my stomach before he pulls my jogging pants down and my knickers with them. Atti doesn't wait as he kisses my core and lifts one of my legs onto his shoulder. The mixture of Atti's tongue and Dabriel's kisses on my neck as his hands slide around my breasts, makes me lose control in seconds. Just before I'm about to finish, Atti stops and looks up at me with a grin.

"Not yet, we have only just started," he says, and they both spend the rest of the day showing me that that was only the start of a long night of pleasure.

CHAPTER 18

"*Elissa, this is the four men I told you about. The wolf, witch, angel, and vampire.*" *Demtra's voice drifts through my mind, and it takes me a few tries to open my eyes and see the massive ballroom we are in where Elissa, the ancestors, and Demtra are all standing together. I recognise the ballroom as the training room now, but it once was amazing. The wall is a shiny gold that matches the glossy, gold floors. There are five crystal chandeliers, lit up with hundreds of candles, the light touching everywhere around the room which is heavily decorated in green flowers. There are hundreds of different supernaturals, dancing in unusual dress to the loud, unfamiliar music being played. The female supernaturals all have white and black Greek-style dresses on, and the men just have togas that cover their lower halves. Their marks are visible as they sway to the music, and I find myself*

admiring the different animals that are also in the room. There are three large, purple birds I've never seen before sitting on a branch by the window, and there are large cats, wolves, bears, and even a horse. The horse is pure white, and as I look closer, I see the horn in the middle of its head. Oh my god, it's a unicorn. I can't believe it.

"May I have a dance with the goddess's sister?" the witch ancestor asks, getting my attention from the unicorn in the room, just in time to see Elissa as she blushes and nods. They walk off and start dancing as I stand and watch. I look over to see all the ancestors watching them, they loved her from the start. It's clear to see in the way they look at her. Demtra walks slowly towards me, and stops so close, I almost imagine she can see me.

"War is coming, the past won't help you now," Demtra says, but her words aren't for me, they are for the demon king who sits at a table behind me. I turn to see the demon king simply smile in a cruel way. Despite the fact he is in the vampire king's body now, he has the same smirk and evil quality in his eyes. It's his soul that screams evil more than anything else.

"The past always controls the future," he replies.

"No, it doesn't, and you won't control her," Demtra says, her voice calm despite her harsh words.

"Gods control all," he sneers before walking away, and I close my eyes as I'm pulled back to sleep.

❄

I blink my eyes open, remembering the dream and how it all started, how my grandmother fell in love with the ancestors, and they loved her. How the demon king was always around, always ruining what could have been special. I guess I should be thankful in a way that he did, because my mum would never have been born if the demon king and Elissa hadn't been together all those years ago. But then, I have to die anyway, so it will all be for nothing. All this death, over many years, will be ended with my death.

"Such a serious face when you first wake up," Dabriel whispers, and I turn my head to see him lying on the bed next to me. I place my hand on his warm, naked chest, tracing my finger around.

"Dreams and war have a way of making me serious," I comment.

"Didn't we help you forget that a little last night?" Atti asks, sliding his hands around my stomach from behind, and I feel how naked he is as he pulls me against him.

"Yes, but we have to plan today, make the hardest decisions for tomorrow," I say, reminding them both of the meeting planned today. I have an idea to tell them, and half my mates are going to hate me for it.

"Then we best get up and be the royals we need to be," Dabriel says and kisses my forehead.

"How are we going to get into the vampire castle and win a fight there?" Lucinda asks, through the noise of everyone trying to shout their ideas into the room. There are sixteen of us in here: the council we have made up to try and win this war. They are a mix of every race and the halves. To say they didn't take it well when Chesca, Soobeen, and Mila walked into the room, despite me warning them this would happen, would be putting it lightly. There was a fight, and Chesca punched one of the witches, it just didn't go well. Luckily, Atti stopped them, but as the shouting gets louder, I know another fight is not far away.

"Enough!" I shout, slamming my hand on the table, and I look down to see my hand glowing blue. I must be glowing like a Smurf again.

"I have an idea," I say and stand up, walking to the whiteboard. I pick up a pen and start drawing while they silently watch me.

"So, you all know that demons can go through the demon ward around the vampire castle. It's how I got out, and it's how I will get in once more. I spoke with Milo, and he will take one person into the castle, and I believe I can pull one person through the ward as well," I say.

"I will go to the vampire castle with Wyatt because he knows it best, and Jaxson because his wolf can smell demons nearby. The rest of the kings and people will stay and fight here," I say, and my mates give me mixed looks of shock and anger.

"No way, Winter," Atti says, his voice dripping with anger.

"I need to close the portal, only me. The demon king is not going to come here and fight. I don't remember much from my time there, but he never left the castle for long because the portal is his weak point. With my crown on, I can fight him, push him in the portal, and close it. This is what I'm meant to do, and I need to," I tell everyone in the room, and there's silence for a long time as they think over my words. I know I don't stand much chance of beating him, but I stand a chance of getting him through that portal, and that's all that matters.

"He could kill you," Dabriel points out.

"I want you all with me, but his demons are

going to kill the people here. Our people," I tell Dabriel, who tightens his jaw but nods. I look over to see Atti finally nod in agreement with me.

"We will take a hundred mixed supernaturals with us, just in case. They can wait outside the castle and, hopefully, kill the rest of the demons he will keep with him when the ward drops. Also, we might need to fight our way to the ward in the first place, if the demon king has any of his demons outside," Jaxson says.

"It's not a bad plan," I comment, agreeing with him.

"Then I will be at your side," Jaxson nods, but the slight glowing of his green eyes is telling me his wolf isn't happy with everything.

"You know my answer," Wyatt says, and I smile at him with relief. I look around the room.

"The Fray are bringing weapons and their army to fight for us, but we cannot trust them. I would suggest placing all the women and children into the castle basement. The rest of you spread out around the castle for the fight," I say.

"We can plan for a war here, My Queen," Lucifer says.

"Then we have our plans. There is a lot still to

be done," Soobeen says, and there's agreements said around the room.

"Winter, you need to see this," Freddy says, running into the room, holding his iPad.

"Freddy, what is it?" I ask, knowing he wouldn't rush in here with just anything. He puts the iPad down on the table, and we all gather around it.

"The wall around Paris has fallen, and whatever happened in there, is not good. I'm fairly sure we are looking at a mass killing of thousands, with thousands still missing. Many were killed in their homes–" the news woman says as she is recorded speaking in front of what is left of Paris. They must be just inside the city, in the streets as some of the houses are on fire, and there are what look like bodies behind her on the street.

"We have a survivor," a woman shouts out, and the camera shakes as they run over the road. A little girl about ten looks into the camera and then at the camera woman.

"Can you tell us who did this?" the woman asks, sliding her arm around the little girl.

"Magic people," she says quietly, but I hear it.

"We are hearing many reports of wolves and witches. Things we only believed existed in fairy tales, but it seems they are real," the camera woman says, and there is silence around the room.

"The government won't hide this, us. This is a mass killing of one of their capitals. They will blame the supernaturals, and humans will hunt us for this," Lucinda says, and I nod my agreement. I don't need to say anything about the humans, as I listen to them rant on about the evil supernaturals. They will never see us as the good guys now.

"You had a witch that can listen for halves and then find them?" I ask Soobeen.

"Yes," Soobeen answers.

"I want you to ask her to put a call out for any supernaturals, tell them that here is safe. When we win the war, we will get Atlantis back, and then we will have two safe havens for supernaturals. And the pack lands at some point," I say, and she nods.

"Yes, My Queen."

"Many supernaturals hide with humans, maybe they will be safe," Atti comments.

"I hope so," I say and look down at the iPad as video recordings of destroyed Paris appear.

Paris is gone.

CHAPTER 19

"*Winter. Winter. Winter!*" *the child-like voice screams in my mind, sounding in pain and making me place my hands on my ears before I even open my eyes. The voice is still screaming as I take in the white, snow-filled field and the one tree in the field that sways in the breeze.*

"So little time left, so much left to fight for," Elissa's kind voice says as she and Demtra walk towards me from behind the tree. Despite her being quite far away, I can hear every word she says. They look like they always do, in white dresses, and when I look down, I see I'm wearing the same. If I dream-call them, why am I dressed like this?

"And it's only you that can win this," Demtra says, her bright eyes locking with mine, and I nod. I know it's only me that can do this, I've known from the second I heard the

prophecy. I have a feeling I've known I'm meant for something my whole life, but I wonder if everyone feels that way?

"When you need us, call us. The power is inside you," *my mother says, stepping out from behind the tree. Her words are spoken in my mind. I watch in silence as I look between them all, all three of them watching me as the snow gets heavier, and I struggle to keep my eyes open.*

"I will win this for you all," I say, my words lost in the cold wind.

"The prophecy was never for anyone other than you, Winter. Only you," Elissa says, and everything turns to white as the snow causes me to close my eyes.

"We need the queen and all of you; the Fray leader is demanding to see the queen and kings," Harris's voice drifts over to me, and I sit up in the empty bed to see Jaxson holding the door open. It's the war today, and when I pull Jaxson's phone off the side to see if we slept in, it's only five in the morning. I groan as I sit up in bed, pulling the sheets closer around myself.

"Fine. Tell the fairy we will be there soon," Jaxson snaps. He is not a morning person, and neither of us got much sleep last night. Both of us are worried about today–the war. It's finally here, and in some ways, I'm glad it is; it means I finally finish this. The prophecy leads us all up to this point, and I don't regret a moment of it. I have my mates because of it, even if my death is the price I have to pay. I would pay it a thousand times for the short time I got with my mates.

"Maybe don't call him a fairy when we meet the leader of the Fray army," I say, laughing a little with Harris before Jaxson slams the door shut.

"They are fairies," Jaxson points out, before rubbing his face. Surprisingly, Jaxson actually put boxers on today, I didn't know he had any here with how often I see his naked butt. Not that I'm complaining, the memory of said butt is kept like a treasure in my mind.

"No, fairies are cute, little things meant for children, with pink, sparkling wings. The Fray queen didn't have wings, and I highly doubt they are all nice and cute," I tell him as he climbs onto the bed and pulls me onto his lap. I press my head into his neck, breathing in his forest-like scent. I love how it makes me feel calm.

"I don't want you to fight him. Every part of me is telling me not to let you go with me. I just can't lose you," Jaxson says gently, kissing his way down my cheek, and I turn my head to meet his lips. Jaxson rolls me onto my back and lowers his body over mine. He kicks his boxers off, pressing himself into me and making me moan slightly.

"You will be at my side," I whisper, breaking away from the kiss.

"I love you, lass. Everything that makes me—well, me—loves you. I don't do romantic words or love poems, but fuck, I would do anything to have a life with you. I was beyond lost until you came into my life. The very thought of letting you fight someone that could kill you—" he says, his voice cracking, and I lean up, kissing him gently again.

"I never did anything, Jaxson. The amazing, strong, and kind man was always there. You never needed me, I was just lucky to have you love me," I say, and he smirks down at me.

"So I didn't put you off with being an idiot at the start?" he asks, and I laugh.

"No, you had me with that first kiss and the jackass behaviour . . . well you're a hot asshole, so I'll forgive you for it," I say, and he grins.

"You're mine, and I'll always be here for you, Winter. No matter what happens today and tonight," he says, resting a hand on my cheek.

"Always," I respond, and he kisses me.

"Sorry to interrupt, but I need to chat with Winter," Wyatt says as he walks into the room and closes the door behind him. Jaxson groans but rolls off me before walking over to the bathroom, naked.

"Clothes, brother," Wyatt says, looking away, and I laugh.

"I'm a wolf, we don't like clothes," Jaxson replies.

"Yes, but the rest of us don't want to see your ass and everything else first thing in the fucking morning," Wyatt shouts as Jaxson shuts the bathroom door, and I laugh even more.

"I like to see you laughing," Wyatt says, and I stand up off the bed. I pull a dressing gown on slowly, watching as his eyes roll over my naked body, and I wish we had more time to explore whatever thoughts are blazing in his dark eyes.

"Morning," I say, walking over, and he kisses me slowly.

"Not that I'm not happy to see you, but I thought you had to meet with the council this morning," I say, knowing they are all meeting very soon, while I'm helping move the women and children to somewhere safe.

"I think we should feed on each other, make us

both as strong as we can be. Blood bags are not a good idea when we are going to fight," Wyatt says gently, and I nod, knowing I need to feed anyway.

"Okay," I say, and he tilts my head to the side, before gently kissing my neck and then biting me. The bite is painful, but only for a second, before nothing but pleasure fills me. I try to keep the moan in by biting my lip, but my teeth are growing sharp in my mouth, so I can't do that. Wyatt licks my neck as he pulls away and then tilts his head to the side. I don't have much control as I lean forward and bite him gently, loving how he tastes like chocolate. His hands tighten on my hips.

When I eventually pull away, he whispers, "We could kick the wolf out and have some fun. I don't have to go to the council meeting straight away."

"The Fray are here, or I would. We have to meet them, and you have to deal with the council before we can all do that," I say, and he groans as he steps away from me.

"I'll meet you later, but I need a minute to calm down," he says, and I see the outline of how turned on he is through his trousers.

"Well, I'm about to strip, so I doubt that will help," I say, and he groans before walking out. I take my time dressing in the leather outfit I have worn to all my fights. It's easy to move in and has places for all my daggers. I leave half my hair down and put the top half up in some plaits. Nothing complicated, but it looks good. When I'm done, Jaxson walks out of the bathroom, fully dressed in jeans and a normal shirt that has a belt around his chest which will hold his sword.

"I'm going to get my weapons." Jaxson says nothing else as he walks out, and leaves the door open. I know that our moment in bed together is over now, and we have to be the royals our people need. They need us to be strong and deal with the Fray. I go over to the box, by the side of my bed, and open it up. The crown calls to me as I pick it up and put it on my head. I walk over to the mirror, seeing myself with the crown on for the first time. I'm slightly glowing blue, and my eyes are brighter than they ever normally are. They have a slight silver quality to them, suggesting they might turn silver at any moment. The crown's power is hard to ignore, but I know I need to.

"My Queen," Atti says as he leans against the wall outside my room. Atti has his own crown on, and his black cloak is covering his clothes. The cloak has silver tree marks stitched down the parting, and he is crossing his arms as he watches me, making his shirt tight on his chest. Atti has shaved his hair on the side of his head, but left the top part long, with his fringe just falling on his forehead. His stormy, grey eyes take their time looking me over.

When he finally gets to my eyes, I say, "My King," with a little bow, and he laughs.

"We sound so formal when all I can think of is shutting this door and fucking you until you scream my name," he tells me. I don't think it's a bad idea at all, and my mark warms on my back as he watches me.

"I don't think we have time," I say with red cheeks, and he chuckles as he walks over to me, pushing my body against the door with his own.

"It's a plan for the future then," he tells me gently before kissing me. Atti moves his lips slowly against mine, and the kiss feels like it's over way too quickly.

"They are waiting, and a fair warning, they are stuck up, rainbow-hair-coloured assholes," Atti says, and I can't help the laugh that escapes my lips.

"'Rainbow-hair-coloured assholes'?" I ask through my laughs, but unfortunately, the door at the bottom of the corridor opens, and one of the said assholes walks over. The man is taller than I am, but I'm short so that's easy, and he has dark blue hair. His eyes match his hair, and I can see flower tattoo-like marks on his neck, which are some kind of blue flower. He has blue eyes that slightly glow, and there's a strange feeling to him that gives him away as a Fray. Another thing is he is extremely hard to look at, he is stunning. Every part of him is extremely beautiful, but in a fake way. It feels like when you eat a chocolate cake that is too rich, and you can't eat all of it.

"I got tired of waiting," he says, his sharp tone means he heard every word. *Way to make alliances, Winter.*

"You should bow," Atti snaps, stopping us from walking closer and puts his arm around me.

"You are not my queen or king," the Fray man snaps out.

"And you are in our home. Sent here to fight for us, so you should show some respect," I say, my tone sharp, and the man's eyes widen as he stares at me, even taking a step back. I glance down to see myself glowing brighter. *Damn, I'm scaring the fairy by glowing like a damn fairy.*

"Are you the leader?" Atti asks with an annoyed sigh as he strokes a hand down my arm, and the man shakes his head. It seems like the Fray man is annoying him.

"Yes. I'm the second in the royal court of the Fray. The queen will not step foot into this world as it makes her weak," the man says, but there's a quiver in his voice.

"Shame. I wanted to speak to Lily," I say, and leave out the fact I want to punch her for tricking me.

"Queen Lilyanne sends her kindness and asked me to say hello to you," he tells me, but I highly doubt she said it nicely, or she isn't as smart as I know she is.

"I'm sure she did," I arch an eyebrow as I speak, and the man nods.

"Why would it make your queen weak to come here?" Atti asks.

"Full-blooded Fray cannot stay in the human world for more than a day, or we start to lose our powers."

"You are being very honest despite working for a queen that is no longer a friend to any of our thrones," Atti replies, tilting his head to the side as he looks at the man.

"What's your name?" I ask him, before the door behind him is opened, and Dabriel comes storming down the corridor. He picks the man up by his neck and slams him into the corridor wall making cracks appear down the newly painted wall. The man squirms, and lightning appears on his fingertips.

"Your people killed one of my angels in a fight. I suggest you deal with them before I start mass killing of Fray," Dabriel says, his marks glowing brightly, and his wings are moving slightly, making him seem like he is floating.

"Y-yes," the man blurts out, and Dabriel lets him drop to the floor.

"Dab?" I ask, and he looks over at me with a kinder smile, but tension is written all over his face.

"The army they promised you is full of untrained soldiers who have no idea what they are doing. The weapons they promised can only be used by people with Fray blood, and most of the soldiers are just picking fights. We had to put a few hundred of them in the dungeons underground, and our supernaturals teamed up to kill a few who flat out wouldn't play nice," Dabriel tells me, shooting a disgusted look at the Fray on the floor.

"What?" I ask, looking down at the man who only stares at the floor.

"The weapons are things like sword handles, which have silver swords come out of them when a Fray touches them. There are strange bracelets and other things I have no clue how to use," Dabriel says.

"Why shouldn't we kill you, send a message back to your queen about how we don't like to be tricked?" Atti says, walking over to stand next to Dabriel, and I wait for the man's answer.

"The army she sent are all prisoners of the Fray war, some may be able to fight, but most are too weak from being kept in the dungeons for years. The queen would never risk her royal army, and she doesn't care about a single Fray here," the man says, his words aimed at the floor as he doesn't look up at us. "Just kill me now if you wish."

"There is a war in Fray?" I ask, ignoring his offer.

"Yes, and there has been for a long time. Ten years ago, Lilyanne made an army. She hunted down every royal Fray and killed them. There is only her left now. We have no choice. My family are being held captive, I have no choice but to do as she asks. When I return to Fray within twenty-four hours, if any of the Fray here come with me, she will kill them all," he tells me, only looking up at me for a second, and the guilt is written all over his face. I believe him when I can see the pain in his eyes, and in some ways, I know Lily is smart enough to do this.

"I believe you, and I won't kill you for telling me the truth. Lily is the only one I want dead right now," I say.

"You say all the royal Fray are dead?" Dabriel asks.

"Yes. I don't know every detail of how the war started as I once was a simple man that lived in the city and worked as a jewel miner. There were once four families for the four royal courts. The autumn court, Lily, is the only one left now," he says.

"Lily made a promise with me, she told me she needed a half-royal Fray that lives in our world."

"Then, there is hope," the man breathes out, and for the first time, there's relief all over his face. "You must never touch the royal Fray, no matter what. She is not safe in my world, but I will return. If the royal ever comes back, I will be there at Lily's side. She needs me to control the miners in the city," he says.

"I will never touch the royal, I never want to make good on my promise," I tell him honestly.

"You may never want to, but magic of the old gods will make the promise come to pass. Promises are always fulfilled," he says, and I just look away from him. I know they have their own gods and their own magic, the lily marks on my wrists are proof of that.

"So, we have thousands of refugees, instead of an army?" I muse, looking through the glass windows just as the sun rises up in the sky.

"Yes," he says.

"Get everyone in front of the castle, so they can see the balcony. All the Fray and supernaturals," I tell the man, who nods and scrambles off the floor, running out as Dabriel still glares at him. I don't see him as a threat to me, but I'm not stupid, I'm going to be careful.

"I will call my witches and ask them to bring everyone as well. I hope you have a plan, or we all need to come up with something quickly," Atti says and presses a kiss against my forehead before he steps away. Dabriel walks over, and I wrap my arms around him.

"I'm sorry about the angels who were killed," I mumble quietly.

"What's the plan?" he asks gently as he pulls me as close as he can to his chest.

"I need to do what I was born for, I need to be a queen," I say, resting my head on his chest.

CHAPTER 20

I look down at the thousands of people on the ground watching me. It's strange to think how many different races there are down there, mixed races, and yes, they all may have differences, but we are here together. All of them are dressed for war, even the women and children are standing with weapons in their hands and determined looks. There are so many people that they stretch out into the forest edges as they wait for me to speak. I try not to remember the human woman who would have laughed if I told her she would be doing this in a year. I'm not her anymore; I'm the queen of four races of people who need my help. They need to see me strong, to remember me like this. Remember me leading them into war for one thing: for peace. For a life for our children.

I glance to the side of the balcony, where Freddy is standing, dressed every bit the prince he is, and the small crown on his head reflecting the sunlight. The sun is high in the sky as everyone looks up at me and my mates. I glance behind me once more to see all four of them standing next to each other, each one looking every bit like the kings they are. Wyatt is the only one without a crown, but he doesn't need it; he commands power on his own, like they all do. The crown is nothing without the powerful king that wears it. *I believe that.* I turn back to the people; the silence is only broken by the cold wind as it blows against the castle. The Fray are standing to the left of the supernaturals, a clear gap between them, and no one seems to want to move. The Fray all have strange, bright coloured hair and old, ragged clothes, and they clutch weapons in their hands. They honestly look terrible, and over half of them must be teenagers or women. There are even some children dotted around, and one woman holding a baby in her arms. Right at the front of the castle is a group of Fray, all big men with determined eyes as they look up at me. A ward is around them, and I know they must be the Fray that started the fights and killed the angels. Not the best way, but then, if they have been kept in dungeons for years, it's likely their families have been too. I know I would do anything to keep my family safe, and I bet they think coming here is just Lily's way of killing them.

"Thank you for coming. For those who do not know who I am, I'm Queen Winter. These are my mates, King Jaxson, King Wyatt, King Dabriel, and King Atticus." I introduce them, and there is silence as I look back at the people. I want to say they can call me Winter and not be formal, but I doubt it's a good idea when I'm trying to get their alliance.

"I have heard that the Fray are at war, a war very much like the one that comes for us today. I'm not going to stand here and ask people who have been kept in dungeons for years to fight for me, for supernaturals whom they don't know, and frankly, don't give a damn about. I'm no fool to ask that of you," I say, my words seeming to be carried by the wind.

"This castle was my grandmother's and my great aunt's. They were goddesses, and my aunt made the first witch, vampire, wolf, and angel. They all lived together in peace in this castle until my grandmother fell in love with a demon. She loved him blindly, and my mother was the only good thing that came from that love. The demon king destroyed this castle, murdered her other mates, and has murdered every blood relative of mine," I say and pause as some of the people start whispering.

"I know the queen of the Fray must have killed some of your family, killed people you love." I tell this to the Fray and then look to the supernaturals.

"The same way the demon king has killed many of our loved ones in this war."

There are mumbles of agreement through the crowd as I wait for them to be a little quieter, so everyone hears my words.

"I'm not going to demand you fight for me, or ask. I only stand here and tell you that I will fight for you. For every single one of you, and the fight is for freedom. No more wars, no more death, and a life for our children!" I shout, and cheers follow my words. I wait for them to calm down before I shout.

"I will kill the demon king and make sure that you are safe. Many of the Fray here may not want to fight, and if you don't, we will keep you safe, regardless, because we are not evil. We are not the bad guy here. We want peace and a safe place for all kinds. It's that or death, and I hope everyone here agrees with me that I choose to fight. But if any of you can fight, please join us," I direct that at the men in the ward, and a few of them nod at me.

"I'm not asking for me, I'm asking for a chance of freedom here. I will welcome you to live here and your children will be taught alongside ours," I say, and I wait for them to say anything. A man steps forward and bows his head, and then another. The rest of the Fray follow and so do the supernaturals.

"Freedom!" Wyatt shouts as he moves next to me.

"For Queen Winter," Dabriel says as he steps forward.

"For those we lost," Jaxson says as he stands next to me, and his hand finds mine.

"And for the future," Atti finally says and steps forward. We all hold hands as the people cheer, and for the first time, we watch as they actually help each other. The first step in creating peace. Now, we need to win the war.

"Be safe," I tell Dabriel, and he gently kisses my nose, making me giggle. Dabriel doesn't need to say any words as we look at each other, all the love he feels for me is written in his eyes. Dabriel only nods before walking away and out the doors of the castle, to his angels to be at their side in the war. I wouldn't expect him to be anywhere else, but worry still fills me when I watch him walk out.

"Queen Winter?" a small, familiar voice says behind me, and I turn to see the half Fray child, Nathaniel.

"Nathaniel, right?" I ask, looking down at him a little. Nathaniel pulls out a dagger from his cloak, the blade is glowing purple, and there's silence around the room as several people stop to stare.

"I can make weapons more powerful than Fray-touched, and I made this for you. I'm not that strong yet, and this took me days. I want to win," Nathaniel says, and I pick the dagger up from him as Soobeen walks over to us. The dagger feels powerful, I can tell. I slide it into a space on my dagger belt.

"Thank you. I won't forget this, and it will help me win," I tell Nathaniel, who shyly nods.

"Nathaniel, we must go," Soobeen says as she wraps an arm around her son.

"You have an amazing son, you must be proud," I say, and Soobeen looks down at her son.

"Very proud," Soobeen says and walks off with her son as I watch.

"Winter?" I hear Alex say, and I look behind me to see her with Drake and Atti. Drake is dressed for war, there is literally no other way to describe him. He has weapons on every single part of his body, and some of them I'm not sure I would even know how to use. They just look like sharp things. A small sob comes from Alex, who wipes her eyes with the men's jumper she has on over her leather leggings.

"You okay?" I ask her, and she nods quickly, putting on a brave smile. I know that smile because it's all I've done all day when I've spoken to anyone. Act brave, or that's what I kept telling myself.

"I can't lose you," she says, and I hug her. I can't give her words of encouragement, not when I know I have to die to close that portal. There isn't another way. I hate that I won't get to meet her little one, but at least I know her child will live. Since Atti saved me, I've tried to swallow the fear and guilt of leaving my mates behind, but I know it's no use. It's me or the rest of the world, and as I pull away and look at Alex, I know she has to survive this. Her baby needs to be born into a good world.

"You go and kill him," Drake says to me, and I nod. Alex kisses my cheek before walking off with Drake. I smile at Harris as he pulls Leigha into a deep kiss by the door. I know they will look after each other.

"Be right back," Atti says and walks a few steps away from me to talk to a couple of witches who seem to be arguing.

"Winter!" I hear Freddy shout and turn to see him running over to me from the stairs. I hold him close as he nearly knocks me over when he gets to me. I pull back when I see his swords strapped to his back, and the reality that he is going to be protecting the women and children with Alex sets in. It's strange that the kids of this war are needed to help, and what childhood Freddy could have had is lost in war. The poor boy has lost so much, and I don't want him to lose anyone else. *I don't want to leave him.*

"You do as Dabriel and Atti ask, okay? I need you to be safe, Freddy," I whisper to him and pull him closer one more time. I don't want anyone else to hear my words.

"I will," he whispers back, and I pull back and look down at him.

"Why do you have your swords on your back, then?" I ask, and he grins.

"Just in case they come near the women and children. I might need to kick some demon—"

"Don't finish that sentence," I say with a laugh, and he grins.

"I'm not a kid, anymore. I haven't been just a kid for a long time," he tells me, and I know he is right, but it doesn't make the situation any better. I hope after all this is done, he can have some part of a childhood again, but I doubt it. He is on the vampire council, and he will be the heir to all of the thrones when I finish this war.

"Just think, this all started with me finding you in that parking lot, another time where you didn't do as you were told," I murmur, and he smiles at me.

"I'm glad you saved me, Winter," he says.

"Me too, Freddy, me too," I say and hug him once more before letting go and having to wipe my eyes a little.

"You can do this, I know it," Freddy tells me, and his bright blue eyes stare up at me.

"I will try," I tell him, and he nods. I look away

for a second as I feel Milo come and sit on my shoulder, and I can't help the chuckle that slips out of my lips when I see Milo's war outfit.

"Dude, we need to work on your fashion sense, I don't even have words for that," Freddy says, and I agree with him as I take in the strange, pink, glittery jumpsuit he has on. There is no way to miss Milo with that outfit and the pink headband in his hair to match.

"You know what?" Freddy tells me.

"What?" I ask.

"You're an awesome stepmum," he says with a cheeky grin and runs off as I laugh. My laugh is cut off when a scream, followed by a loud bang comes from outside. I feel Milo hold onto my neck as I step backwards as the castle shakes a little. There's more sounds of screams, and all the people in here run outside. I look over as Wyatt and Jaxson run down the stairs, both of them have their swords strapped on their backs and are wearing tight clothes in black. Jaxson's crown makes him seem like he is lightly glowing, and Wyatt is oozing power as they run over to me.

"It's time to go," Atti says walking to my side, and he links his fingers with mine as Wyatt and Jaxson run over to us. I duck as a demon comes flying through the door, and lands in the entrance hall. I pull a dagger out of my belt and throw it at his head, watching as it hits, and the demon disappears into blue dust. I hear a scream and turn to see Leigha fighting three demons who must have snuck in somehow, with Alex behind her. I go to step forward when Harris runs past me.

"Wait, we need the hundred people we are meant to be taking with us," I say to Atti, and he shakes his head.

"They came too early, we need to go now. We can't afford to wait, Winter," he says, and I look back at Alex, Leigha, and Freddy, wanting to help them.

"Go, I will sort them," Harris shouts at us as he runs towards Alex, and Leigha follows him, with a small nod at me as she passes. I feel Atti's magic pulling us away only a second later.

CHAPTER 21

"**W**e're here," Wyatt says as I open my eyes to the vampire castle. It's snowing, and the large flakes of snow land on my face as the cold wind blows it around us. It's almost fitting that it's winter, and there is so much snow. Like my namesake being Winter, I've always loved the cold and the snow. I wonder if that's why there is always snow in my dreams with my family, because I subconsciously chose it. We walk in silence towards the castle, listening for any sounds, but there is nothing. It's eerily quiet here.

"Come, vampire," Milo says, and I look up as the blue ward surrounding the vampire castle comes into view. No one says anything about the fact the demon has moved it beyond the wall, and I hope it's not because he has demons just waiting for us behind it. Milo flies off my shoulder and lands on Wyatt's shoulder. I look up at Atti, who leans down and kisses me.

"Go and kill him," he tells me firmly.

"Save our people and know I love you so much," I tell him, trying to keep my voice stronger, and he pulls me into a deep kiss before breaking away. I watch as he disappears. I love that he believes in me, there wasn't a bit of doubt in his voice, and that kiss was what I want to remember as I walk into this castle. As I literally try to send a demon back to hell.

"Lass?" Jaxson says gently, and I wipe some of the snow out my eyes as I look up at him.

"Let's go," I say and link my hands with Jaxson's as we walk up to the ward. The ward is as deep as I remember it being, but there's something strange about it, like it's weaker. I walk straight through it and pull Jaxson with me. It's easier to travel through the second time than it was the first, even pulling Jaxson with me. My spare hand goes to one of my daggers as I take in the imposing wall and wipe more of the snow out of my eyes with the back of my hand. There are no demons around, and Jaxson nods down at me, he can't sense any either. I wait as Milo leads Wyatt through after us only moments later, and Wyatt looks around.

"We need to jump," I say, wondering how Jaxson will make that jump. I know Atti used his air power to help boost him, and Wyatt won't have an issue because of him being a vampire.

"No, we don't. I know a way in," Wyatt tells us. "Come on, we'd better get inside, in case there is a patrol."

We follow Wyatt as he walks next to the wall for about ten minutes before he stops and holds his hand up. Wyatt pushes against what looks like the rest of the castle wall, but it moves inwards at his push. The wall slides to the left, and Wyatt walks into the dark room. *That's a cool secret door.* When I step forward, I notice it's not a room at all, it's a corridor. The dark corridor is impossible to see down, and the strong smell of damp fills my senses. Wyatt gets his phone out, using the light, so we can see down the now creepy, cobweb-filled corridor.

"I won't shift unless we need to fight, I can use my sword if there are only a few," Jaxson whispers gently.

"You should try not to use your power inside, the castle is old and won't last through an earthquake," Wyatt warns Jaxson, who nods. He has a point; the castle is ancient and made out of stone.

"Okay, but can you smell any coming near us in your human from?" I ask Jaxson.

"Yes, they smell like death. It's not hard to miss," Jaxson says.

"Milo, you need to stay here. You can't come with us here."

"Live, you family," Milo tells me, making me want to cry, but I put on a brave face as he kisses my cheek and then flies to sit on a ledge just inside the corridor. I know any demons won't hurt him if they find him, he is part demon after all. Wyatt looks back at us for a second before he keeps walking down the long corridor. I remember what they smell like, and how the dead bodies they inhabit seem to be dying anyway. *I wonder how long it would take for the bodies they have to die? Do they just find a new body until all the people on earth are dead or demons?*

"This opens up just outside the throne room, where the ball was held, and the portal is open. That's why I chose this one," Wyatt tells us as we keep walking, and the corridor takes a left.

"Hopefully he is there."

"The portal is weak today, just like the castle ward. All ward and portal magic is weak today,"

Jaxson tells me, and I don't question how he knows. Everyone has been researching and finding out all they could to help us. I'm sure someone found this out for him. It seems like forever that we walk in silence, with the dripping water and our breaths being the only sounds.

"I can smell some close," Jaxson tells us, and Wyatt stops at the same time I do. I don't think they are close, but there is a faint smell of death.

"The door is right there," Wyatt says and points up with his light. There's a small hole and a long ladder to climb up. Wyatt pulls the creaky old ladder down quietly with the long handle, and then we wait for a second to see if anyone heard us. When nothing happens, we all take a deep breath. This whole plan banks on the demon king not being ready for us. If he caught us down here, we would have a disadvantage.

"Hold the light," Wyatt says, and hands me his phone. He pulls his sword out from its holder and starts climbing the ladder. Jaxson follows after him, and I hold the light until Wyatt opens the door. The light from the door fills the tunnel, and I quickly drop Wyatt's phone into one of my pockets and start climbing. I hear Jaxson's growl, and then the castle shakes slightly, making me nearly fall off the ladder, but I manage to hold on. When I finally get to the top, Wyatt and Jaxson are fighting dozens of demons. Wyatt is using both his swords to fight and behead demon after demon. Jaxson is doing the same with his large sword, both of them glancing over at me. I don't have time to look again as three demons run at me with silver swords. I pull my power and send them flying, both of them disappearing into dust, and I pull a dagger out of my belt, throwing it at a demon at Jaxson's back. The whole corridor is full of demons, there are far too many for us. I pull another dagger out and throw it at a demon running at me, and the moment it hits its head, it disappears into dust. The demon king was waiting for us.

"All fun, isn't it?" the demon king's laugh comes from behind me, and I turn to see him leaning against the entrance to the throne room. He has a long cloak on as well as the vampire crown that belongs to Wyatt, and his red eyes meet mine. In so many ways I hate that I'm related to him, that I share his blood, and that I have to be the one to fight him. I hate that he tricked the vampire king into bringing him back, I hate everything about this man.

"Why?" he asks, tilting his head to the side as I

walk over to him. I keep my eyes on him as I call my power and kill two demons with a wave as they run at me.

"Family treasures. Seems you don't know everything, demon," I respond drily.

"Well, well . . . my princess isn't stupid after all," he says, looking at my crown, and then he turns and walks back into the throne room. I run after him, surprised that no demons try to attack me as they seem to let me pass. The demon king is standing in the middle of the throne room when I run in, the portal is still open and takes up the entire side wall now. It's getting bigger, and it's hard to take my eyes off it. It almost calls to me, as I can feel its power from here.

"Let me guess, you came to put me back in the demon realm forever?" he laughs as he speaks. "Your dead great-aunt tricked me once, but I am done being tricked."

"Yes, but it will be no trick. You will die in that realm, in hell, where you belong," I respond. I don't need to look down as I feel my crown's power stretch though my body.

"You're not strong enough." He laughs, and the castle shakes hard, knocking us both to the floor with a bang. I look up as I roll across the floor, seeing the large cracks going up the ceiling, and the ground keeps shaking. I call my power, using the crown's power to make it stronger and stand up on the shaky ground. The demon king is just standing up, an annoyed look on his face.

"Stupid wolf," he says with anger, walking away from me and towards the door to my mates. I won't let that happen.

"Then fight me and see who wins. See who deserves to rule and who truly has the blood of a goddess," I shout, knowing from my dreams that he believes he is truly one when he is not. He turns to face me with a slow smirk.

"Don't cry when I kill you, at least die like a real demon princess," he says, and I don't waste time listening to him as I shoot a wave of my blue power at him as the ground shakes harder, and the room seems to almost tilt to the side. I look up to see him walking over to me as he avoids pieces of stone that fall from the cracked ceiling He sends his own wave of red power towards my wave as he walks, and when the waves meet, it sends a shock wave that sends me flying across the room. I manage to land on my side and quickly get up, calling my power again, and he does the same, shooting a long stream of power at me. I copy what he does, trying to hold my power against his, but it doesn't work for long. Another shockwave fills the room, and I scream as pieces of stone fall from the ceiling and one hits my shoulder. This time, I fly into the wall and my head bangs against it. I pick the Fray-touched dagger out of my belt, but the demon king leans down, taking it out of my hand before I can throw it. He looks at the dagger and laughs, before sliding it into his pocket as I try to get up, and everything goes blurry.

"Silly princess to think you could kill me. You know, I never wanted to kill you, I wanted you to rule at my side. My only family left, and you betray me. I'm four times more powerful than you are, and all I have to do is get that silly crown off you and then order you to go and kill your mates," he says and leans down to touch the crown.

"Winter!" I hear Wyatt shout.

CHAPTER 22

ATTICUS

"Watch out!" I shout as three demons run at an angel who is picking a woman up off the floor. I call my fire, but I'm too late to stop one of the demons running a silver sword through the back of the angel. He screams out in pain, the scream mixing with everyone else's on the battlefield outside the castle, and I kill the demons with my fire. The angel I recognise as Chesca flies down from the sky and stands in front of the woman on the floor, and nods at me. She is going to protect the woman. I turn and look around the battlefield outside the castle, which is littered with supernaturals bodies, demons running around with silver weapons, and angels are flying in the skies overhead.

"No!" I scream as a demon rips the head off a wolf with his bare hands, and another, smaller, female wolf runs towards the demon. I pull my air power and hold the demon in place as the female wolf jumps and rips the head off the demon and lands on the ground. I don't have long to see if she is okay as a ball of fire flies past me, and I jump out of the way.

"Atti!" I hear shouted behind me, but when I turn around in a circle, I can't see who shouted at me. I turn just in time to see a Fray lift his hands in the air, and, to my shock, a tornado appears in his hand. The Fray with green hair throws the tornado towards the demons running towards us, and it gets bigger as they run straight into it. Another Fray woman runs up next to me and puts her hands into the air. Rain pours down on us as dark clouds fill the skies. I watch as she redirects some of the rain, turning it into sharp icicles and shooting them into five demons' necks in one go.

"Weather magic, that's what you can do?" I ask her, and she nods. A loud roar fills the night as I feel a big intrusion to the ward. The demons can just walk straight through it. It must be something to do with the Winter solstice, but I doubt we will ever know. After the roar, a lot of people stop but not for long, as the demons don't seem to notice. The tornado is pulling the air from the ground, and it feels like I'm being suffocated as I look up into the dark skies.

"Demon," the woman screams next to me and points up to the sky. The dragon that Winter set free flies across the woods and shoots blue fire into the tornadoes. It suddenly comes back to me what Milo said about dragons. He must have called the dragon here.

"Dragons, Milo, seriously?" I mutter, knowing tornadoes mixed with dragons is just as dangerous to us, as well as the demons. I glance over to see Dabriel fighting with four demons, and I know I need to help, now. I run over and use my air to send two of the demons flying away into the tornado. By the time I get to Dabriel, he has killed the other two, and all that is left is dust.

"That is not helping us," Dabriel points at the dragon, which is setting half the woods on fire and randomly flying down and picking demons up, throwing them into the fire.

"Freddy!" Dabriel shouts, and I turn to see where he is looking. Freddy and a silver wolf are surrounded by at least ten demons. The wolf is injured, and Freddy is protecting him.

"No!" I shout when the demons block my view of Freddy, and I run over to them. I burn all the demons in my path, and see Dabriel flying ahead towards Freddy. Winter could never live with herself if she lost Freddy, none of us could. The little shit is family to us, and he needs to live, so I can kill him myself for being out here fighting.

"Duck," I shout at Freddy when I get through the demons and see Freddy is fighting with one. Freddy does as I ask, and I lift both my hands, calling air and lifting all the demons around me into the air. Dabriel flies around and kills each one before landing next to Freddy.

"I'm fine," Freddy says, holding his arm that is bleeding.

"What the fuck are you doing out here?" I shout at him, picking up the sword he had dropped and giving it to him.

"Mich needed me," he nods towards the injured wolf.

"Get inside," I say, and he nods. I go to take him and Mich back when the dragon roars loudly, and I look up just in time to feel two more large things pass through the ward that is connected to my magic. Even now, the crystal is trying to fight for us. I watch the skies and two more dragons appear in the distance. The dragons roar at each other, and the tornadoes are making it difficult to see them, but the fire they shoot is killing everyone on the ground.

"They will destroy everything in this fight," I shout at Dabriel and hear a scream behind me. I turn around to see Lucifer holding his chest, a sword in the middle of his chest, and he falls to the ground. The demon behind him pulls the sword out of Lucifer's chest, and I shoot my fire at him, burning the demon to pieces as we all run over.

"Lucifer," Dabriel says as he pulls Lucifer's shirt up and tries to heal him.

"Tell Josh–" Lucifer says but doesn't finish his sentence as he coughs on blood, and his head drops to the side. Dabriel just stares down at him, his hands still on his chest.

"Dabriel . . . he is gone," I say, shaking his shoulder and needing him to get out of his shock. Dabriel stands up and nods, lifting his sword and standing in front of Freddy and Mich's wolf.

"Get everyone inside the castle, now," I shout and use my powers to send the message to all the witches.

I wrap an arm around Freddy and Mich, and Dabriel puts his hand on my shoulder before I move us all inside the castle. The castle shakes as we get inside, and I run back to the door with Dabriel at my side. The dragons' roars are loud enough to shake the castle, let alone their fight. I only hope Winter's dragon is strong enough to kill the others and take the demons with him.

"We fight together, brother, and save as many as we can," Dabriel says.

"Together," I say, and we run out into the battle as our people run inside.

CHAPTER 23

WYATT

I swing one of my swords down over the head of the final demon in front of me as the castle shakes. I turn to see Jaxson has killed his demons but destroyed the castle as he has been using his power. The castle shakes, sending all of us flying into the side of the corridor, and the remaining demons that are running towards us go flying through one of the doors in the room. A loud scream makes me stand up as quick as I can.

"Winter!" I shout when I hear her scream again, and this time it sounds more desperate than before. I run into the throne room with Jaxson following to see Winter on the ground, holding the crown in her hands as the demon king tries to pull it off her. I know if he gets that crown off her, he will control her, but I won't let that happen again.

"I will cut your hands off, little princess," the demon king warns, and I run over to him as he turns to see me.

"Ah, the vampire comes to save little Winter," he laughs, letting go of the crown, and Winter falls to the ground. I look her over quickly, seeing the blood on her head and the cut that is healing, but otherwise, she looks okay. She is alive, at least.

"I've come for my queen and my crown," I nod my head towards the crown he is wearing that belongs to me. That crown has always been worn by the king of the vampires, and despite hating my father and the royal family I was born into, the crown is mine.

"You vampires are always fun to kill." He laughs. I chuck one of my swords over to him, and he catches it.

"Fair fight," I say, and he nods with a smirk. Jaxson runs into the room and over to Winter, and I see him from the corner of my eye, but I don't take my eyes off the demon king as he looks over at Winter.

"Wolfy has come to die, too? I have to say, your ancestor was the best one to kill. So easy," he says, and Jaxson's growl fills the room, causing another shake of the castle which almost makes me fall over. I hold my ground like the demon king does as he turns his evil, red eyes on me.

"I'm a demon, I don't play fair, so don't expect it, boy," he shrugs, looking every bit like my father as he does.

"Good thing I don't either," I say and use my vampire speed to rush at him, catching him off guard a little and cutting his side. He swings around, and I block with my own sword as he throws hit after hit, and I block him. He shocks me by using a red wave of his power, but my sword blocks it, cutting through the wave. His eyes widen as he takes in my Fray-touched sword, one that Freddy had his friend make for me. I manage to get him back across the room towards the portal with the fifth hit. He knows it by the evil smirk he gives me as our swords clash, and he throws wave after wave of red power between the hits. I look over to see Jaxson holding Winter as she screams for him to let her go and to help me. Her blue eyes meet mine, filled with worry, but I look away before I can feel any guilt for not spending more time with her. For not telling her what I planned today.

I focus back on the demon king, his red eyes

bright with power as he hits my sword again with a big bang, and I twist, so my back is towards the portal. The coldness of the portal hits my back as I'm pushed against it with every hit of our swords. I hit him once more, but this time jump off the ground, catapulting over him and slam my legs into his back. He looks on in shock as I send him flying against the ground in front of the portal, and his sword falls into the portal. I run after him and pick him up, pushing him into the blue portal with both my hands. I pull the crown off his head quickly with one hand, as he struggles to hold onto my other hand that is pushing him further into the portal. I edge my feet closer, knowing he could easily pull me in with him at this point.

"If I'm going, then so are you," he says as he struggles against me, and I push once more and let go, as I feel a sharp pain through my heart. The demon king laughs as he disappears into the portal, and I look down at the silver dagger in my heart.

"**N**o, it can't be that," *Dabriel says, standing up from the chair he is sitting on in the meeting room. Atti and Jaxson look at me in shock, not expecting me to tell them this when I asked to speak to them all before the war tomorrow. I called this meeting because Winter has to survive, nothing else matters to me, and I know they feel the same way. I never expected to fall for her, to love her more than myself.*

"Listen to the prophecy: the words. I know it's me. I saved her, I brought her back to life. I'm her saviour," I tell Jaxson. I don't need to convince them what I already know.

"It's bullshit and doesn't mean anything. I'm not losing you because of some old prophecy, not after everything we have been through," Atti snaps out.

"The blue-sided human will choose a side.
When four princes are born on the same day, they will rule true.
Her saviour will die when the choice is made.
If she chooses wrong, she will fall.
If she chooses right, then she will rule.
Only her mates can stop her from the destruction of all.
If the fates allow, no one need fall.
For only the true kings hold her fate, and they will be her

mates." I repeat the prophecy to them all, and they silently watch me.

"Every part of the prophecy has already come true. We were born on the same day, she chose right and rules all races. We as her mates stopped her from destroying everything with the demon king..." I say and clear my throat. "To close the portal, someone of her blood must die. I can feed on her and have her blood. I'm her saviour, and I will die for her." I finish my sentence, and Jaxson punches the wall next to him. Atti looks up at the ceiling, and Dabriel looks down at the ground. There aren't many words that can be said, nothing will change what has to happen. It will be me or her, and I'm going to make sure it's me. I just hope she knows the strength of my love for her, it's everything to me.

"Did you always know?" Atti asks me quietly, a look of shock on his face as he meets my gaze. His voice sounds like he has given up all hope, and he finally understands how I've been feeling for a long time.

"No. Not at first. I realised when she came back to life, and I had saved her," I tell him. I remember when I walked into the bedroom and saw her awake on my bed. I remember kissing her as I realised that I saved her and what that meant. Every part of me wanted to run away until she woke up, and then I knew, I knew I'd never leave her. If it meant death,

then that was the price I'd willingly pay for my time with her. I never had true happiness, not with anyone, until her.

"That's a long time to know," Jaxson practically growls and starts pacing the room.

"The prophecy still says, 'If the fates allow, no one need fall,'" Dabriel says. *I know that part of the prophecy, but I doubt fate can save me now.*

"Tomorrow, you need to get Winter out of the way," I tell Jaxson, who stops pacing and rubs his face with his hands.

"She will hate me for not stopping you. She will hate us all for knowing. We have to tell her," Jaxson says.

"If you tell her, she will never let me in the castle. She would die to save us all."

"I think that's been her plan all along," Atti says quietly.

"I want her alive, but this is too much, what you're asking for," Dabriel says, shaking his head.

"Let's put this simply, if any of you could die to save her, would you?" I ask them, and they don't say anything, which is the answer I needed.

"She will be alive, that's all that matters to me. Let me do this," I say. Jaxson's simple nod is all I need as an answer from him.

"Fine," Atti responds.

"The fates will stop this, no one is cruel enough to do this," Dabriel says, but I know from how he looks at me that *he won't say anything. Winter is everything to us all, and we won't risk her life.*

"NO!" Winter screams behind me, but I watch as my blood, mixed with Winter's, drops onto the portal, and it cracks. The portal slowly disappears as I fall to my knees, nothing else matters now. *I saved her.*

CHAPTER 24

"*L*et me go, Jaxson," I struggle against him as he holds me close, and I watch Wyatt push the demon king into the portal. The demon king says something to him, just as he falls into the portal and is too far inside to get out. *He did it.* I need to put my blood on the portal now and close it, ending this all. I have to die, or it can be opened again. All these thoughts rush through my mind as I continue to struggle in Jaxson's arms, and then I see the dagger. The demon king slides a dagger straight into Wyatt's chest and then falls into the portal. The portal cracks and closes when it hits me: Wyatt is my saviour, and he fed on me, he has my blood. His death will close the portal.

"NO!" I shout, and Jaxson lets me go as the

portal disappears completely, and Wyatt falls to his knees. I run over the broken stone covering the floor and avoid the bits that are still falling as the castle shakes, and I catch him just as he falls back, laying his head on my lap.

"Don't do this, please, God, no!" I scream, holding my hand over the dagger and pulling it out. I look at the blood-covered dagger, seeing it's the one Nathaniel made me. The dagger I tried to use on the demon king and he used to hurt Wyatt instead. I drop the dagger in shock. I place my hand on his chest and look over to Jaxson who kneels on the other side of Wyatt.

"DO SOMETHING!" I shout at him with tears running down my face, "Please," I beg, and he shakes his head as he bows his head.

"Nothing I can do, lass. I would save my brother if I could," he says, and I shake my head.

"Winter," Wyatt groans my name, his word mixed with pain as I look down at him.

"You cannot die . . . I love you so much. We have years left together, and children. I want my life with you," I say, my voice catching as I start crying harder.

"Dad!" I hear Freddy scream behind me, and I turn my head to see him running over with Dabriel and Atti following. They fall to their knees around Wyatt as I gently push a piece of his hair off his forehead with shaky hands.

"Heal him," I beg Dabriel, and he puts his hands on Wyatt's chest. Dabriel glows brightly for a few minutes before he takes his hands away and shakes his head.

"No, no, no, no," I mumble and hold Wyatt as close as I can.

"Thank you for being in my life, for saving Freddy, and for letting me love you. I would die over and over for you, Winter," he says as black lines crawl up his neck and cover his face. His dark eyes close, and I can't control the half sob and scream that escapes my lips.

"DEMTRA! ELISSA! MOTHER!" I scream their names again and again into the silent room as pain fills my body, and I close my eyes, resting my head on Wyatt's cold one. I can feel the emptiness of his loss, and the pain is overwhelming in my chest as waves of pain crash through me. They can't let it end like this, not like this. I don't want to live without him, not when he died for me. My mate. My saviour. My love.

"Come to me, help me now. I need you, I need

my family to help me now and will never call you again," I whisper, and that's when I feel it. A coldness and stillness to the room that makes me look up. The castle has stopped shaking, and the room is still while snow falls through the hole in the ceiling onto us. Jaxson's wide eyes meet mine as I look around, and he nods behind me. I look behind me to see three, white, ghost-like figures, which gradually come into view as Elissa, Demtra, and my mother. All three of them have the white dresses on from my dreams, and it's Demtra that moves close to me.

"Do you know another name for a goddess?" Demtra asks me, her voice is gentle and kind as my heart begins to fill with hope.

"No," I whisper as the others move away, so Demtra can kneel where Jaxson once was. They all look at her in shock before bowing their heads, even Freddy does as he shifts into a wolf, losing whatever control he had over his emotions.

"Fates," she says.

"If the fates allow, no one need fall," Atti whispers the line of the prophecy for all of us to hear, and Freddy's wolf howls into the night. The howl is full of hope, much like what is filling my chest as I watch my family. I don't take my eyes off Demtra as my mother and Elissa move to her side. They both place a hand on her shoulders.

"The vampires have the mark of a phoenix for a reason, sweet Winter. Phoenixes are reborn," Demtra says and places both her hands on Wyatt's stomach. The black lines slowly disappear before he takes a deep breath, and his dark eyes open, locking onto mine.

"Wyatt . . . Wyatt, oh my God," I sob out in between tears as he sits up and pulls me into his arms. I look over Wyatt's shoulder to see all three of them standing close together and watching us.

"It's our time to rest and your time to rule; this is your fate, Queen Winter," Elissa says gently before she and Demtra disappear into the snow that fills the room. I lock eyes with my mother, and I know this is the last time I'm going to see her.

"Thank you, and I love you, Mum," I say in a whisper, but her whole face lights up.

"We are so proud of you, our Winter," my mother whispers as she disappears too, and my breath catches in my throat. I feel my other mates kneel next to us. None of us move for a long time.

"We won," Atti finally says into the silence of the snow-filled, destroyed room.

Yes, we did.

"Is the castle safe?" I ask as Freddy's wolf comes and places his head on Wyatt's lap. Wyatt strokes his head as Freddy whines.

"Yes, your dragon turned up, and the Fray created some tornadoes . . ."

"Tornadoes and dragons . . . is anyone else alive?"

"Yes, we saved a lot of people, and the demons are dead. Harris is leading some fighters to check the rest, and the angels are now healing everyone. We won," Dabriel answers for me. I don't respond as Wyatt gently tilts my face to his, and brushes his lips against mine. I feel nothing but relief and happiness through my bond from all of them.

"It's over," I whisper, and everyone hears my words.

EPILOGUE

"*Where* was I?" I ask as I finish feeding the baby in my arms her bottle of milk. I place the bottle on the bench next to me and carry on my story.

"We won the battle against the bad king of demons, and the big dragon that lives in the mountains now killed the other bad dragons and demons here. There were many brave people lost in the war, but they will never be forgotten. Now, we live in peace, with cute little babies everywhere like you," I tell Ella, as I rock her in my arms, and she looks up at me. Not that she understands a single word I'm saying, as she is two months old. I glance up at my home, the goddess's castle, and see how it looks far better since the war. The dragons destroyed a lot of it, so we had to build again, but it didn't matter to us. The only thing that mattered was the fact that most of the supernaturals got inside the castle and to the underground dungeons before the massive dragon fight. I wish I could say thank you to my dragon that won. He lives in one of the mountains around the castle, and we see him fly over the castle at times. He is like our protector now.

The castle has been made more modern while we did the fixes it needed. There is a lot we had to deal with, like the humans who now hunt our kind or anything that seems supernatural since the war. The governments have an order to kill any supernaturals they find, but our witches send out messages to any stray supernaturals to come here and we will keep them safe. I hate that our people can't be safe everywhere anymore, but it's not something I can change. We have the witches' city back, after a long time of building new wards around it and safely removing the humans who found the island.

"I doubt the stories of how the war was won are the best kind of baby story to help my daughter sleep," Alex says as she walks over to me. I glance up at my best friend as she laughs at me.

"I didn't know what to say to a baby. Everyone

keeps handing me babies and expecting me to know what to do." I laugh as I hand over her daughter to her.

"Well, auntie Winter, maybe try fairy tales next time," she says. I guess that makes sense.

"Like the big bad wolf?" I joke, and she laughs.

"Speaking of wolves, your mates want you. They're waiting outside the castle," she says, and I stand up from the bench I was sitting on.

"Alright," I say and kiss her cheek before walking back through the newly planted trees that lead to the castle. My mates are sitting on the bottom steps. Wyatt is laughing with Jaxson over something, and Dabriel is looking at something on Atti's phone. For the first few months after nearly losing Wyatt, I never let him out my sight. I kept all my mates close as we rebuilt everything we lost in the war. I wasn't happy that Wyatt died for me and that my other mates knew, but then, I was prepared to do the same sacrifice for him. In the end, we all love each other that much that we want to make sure we all live. I don't see how that can be considered a bad thing. I look over to see Dabriel straighten up, his eyes going white like he does when he has a vision. I run over and stop in front of him, all of us silent as we wait for him to come back from the vision. When his purple eyes come into focus, he looks down at me, and I take his hand in mine.

"Adelaide," he whispers, and I frown at him.

"Who is that?" I ask, considering it's an unusual name, and I think I would remember it.

"The Fray you will meet. I saw you shaking hands with her and someone else saying 'this is Adelaide,' and then what looked like a portal opened," he tells me.

"How did you know she is the Fray child?" I ask him, hoping for any way to get out of this vision being right.

"I could see her aura, it was so red and bright. It looked just like a Fray's, and I doubt a portal would open for anyone other than the royal," he tells me, and I nod, letting him pull me into his arms. I feel sick at the idea of Lily being anywhere near Adelaide, even if I don't know her. I have spoken to many of the Fray that survived the wars, and they all speak only of her cruelness. They say she is an insane queen that is touched by the God of Death, but I don't understand their gods enough to make sense of that. All the Fray are slowly losing their powers now, and they say it is what they want, but I still feel sorry for them.

"We will worry about the promise another day, we can't do anything about it now," I say after a long pause, and he sighs.

"That is true," he leans down and gently kisses me.

"I heard you all wanted me?" I ask, and he smiles.

"We found something and want to show you," Atti says and links my other hand in his. We walk around the castle, where we pass the outside training area. Freddy and Nathaniel are training, both of them circling each other with swords. Mich and Josh are watching from the sides and drinking water. It's good to see them all together, all friends. It's like what my mates had with each other growing up.

"They have gotten close since the war. Freddy told me that Mich, Josh, and Nath saved him, and that's how Mich ended up getting hurt in the war," Wyatt tells us. Wyatt and Freddy have gotten closer, too, and I couldn't be happier to see that change come about. Freddy actually calls him Dad since the war. I think losing Wyatt for that brief time made Freddy realise how much he actually loves Wyatt, but he wouldn't admit that out loud to us. Stroppy teenage hormones and all that. Josh waves as we walk past, and I wave back. I was sad to learn of Lucifer's death in the war, and I'm keeping my promise to bring Josh up. I moved him into Freddy's room, and now he is part of my family, despite the fact Josh doesn't speak to us much, and I have no idea what he is.

"So, why are we going into the woods?" I ask, trying to distract myself as we take a path into the woods to the left of the castle, where I have never been before.

"It's a surprise," Atti laughs.

"You know I don't like surprises, unless they are chocolate-covered," I say, making them all laugh, but I'm being deadly serious. A chocolate surprise is always a good one. We walk around the woods for a little while before we get to a lake that is hidden within the trees. You couldn't see it from the castle before, but now that some of the trees were burnt down, the sun is shining down on the lake, and it's really beautiful here. I think it's the calmness of the water and the way it feels like you're away from the world here.

"It's beautiful here," I comment, looking up as Dabriel pulls me to his chest.

"You remember that vision I had of us all by a

lake, and Freddy was much older? The one I told you about once," Dabriel asks me.

"I remember. Was it here?" I ask, knowing that Dabriel said he felt complete in the vision. Much like I do now with all my mates when war isn't chasing us, and we have our lives to enjoy.

"Yes, and I didn't tell you something about that vision," he says, and I pull away a little to look up at him.

"What was it?"

"You. You were pregnant in that vision, Winter," he tells me, and I lean up and kiss him, knowing we will have our future we fought for. *It was worth all this.* I lean back and catch a glance of three figures in white dresses floating in the middle of the lake, feeling their love from here.

This was my fate and my future, with all my mates.

The End For Now. Continuing Reading in this world with Wings Of Ice.

AUTHORS NOTE

Hello and thank you for buying my book! You're amazing, and I can't tell you how much I appreciate your support.

A big thank you to Michelle, Helayna Taylor, Anna, and Meagan.

Thank you to all my family for their support as I wrote this book. Thank you to my husband for feeding me when I forgot to eat and my children for not destroying the house.

DESCRIPTION

I knew nothing about mates until the alpha rejected me...

Growing up in one of the biggest packs in the world, I have my life planned out for me from the second I turn eighteen and find my true mate in the moon ceremony.

Finding your true mate gives you the power to share the shifter energy they have, given to the males of the pack by the moon goddess herself. The power to shift into a wolf.

But for the first time in the history of our pack, the new alpha is mated with a nobody. A foster kid living in the pack's orphanage with no ancestors or power to claim.

Me.

After being brutally rejected by my alpha mate, publicly humiliated and thrown away into the sea, the dark wolves of the Fall Mountain Pack find me.

They save me. The four alphas. The ones the world
fears because of the darkness they live in.
In their world? Being rejected is the only way to join
their pack. The only way their lost and forbidden
god gives them the power to shift without a mate.

I spent my life worshipping the moon goddess,
when it turns out my life always belonged to
another...

*This is a full-length reverse harem romance novel full of sexy
alpha males, steamy scenes, a strong heroine and a lot of
sarcasm. Intended for 17+ readers. This is a trilogy.*

CHAPTER

ONE

"*D*on't hide from us, little pup. Don't you want to play with the wolves?"

Beta Valeriu's voice rings out around me as I duck under the staircase of the empty house, dodging a few cobwebs that get trapped in my long blonde hair. Breathlessly, I sink to the floor and wrap my arms around my legs, trying not to breathe in the thick scent of damp and dust. Closing my eyes, I pray to the moon goddess that they will get bored with chasing me, but I know better. No goddess is going to save my ass tonight. Not when I'm being hunted by literal wolves.

I made a mistake. A big mistake. I went to a party in the pack, like all my other classmates at the beta's house, to celebrate the end of our schooling and, personally for me, turning eighteen. For some tiny reason, I thought I could be normal for one night. Be like them.

And not just one of the foster kids the pack

keeps alive because of the laws put in place by a goddess no one has seen in hundreds of years. I should have known the betas in training would get drunk and decide chasing me for another one of their "fun" beatings would be a good way to prove themselves.

Wiping the blood from my bottom lip where one of them caught me in the forest with his fist, I stare at my blood-tipped fingers in a beam of moonlight shining through the broken panelled wall behind me.

I don't know why I think anyone is going to save me. I'm nothing to them, the pack, or to the moon goddess I pray to every night like everyone in this pack does.

The moon goddess hasn't saved me from shit.

Heavy footsteps echo closer, changing from crunching leaves to hitting concrete floor, and I know they are in the house now. A rat runs past my leg, and I nearly scream as I jolt backwards into a loose metal panel that vibrates, the metal smacking against another piece and revealing my location to the wolves hunting me.

Crap.

My hands shake as I climb to my feet and slowly step out into the middle of the room as Beta

Valeriu comes in with his two sidekicks, who stumble to his side. I glance around the room, seeing the staircase is broken and there is an enormous gap on the second floor. It looks burnt out from a fire, but there is no other exit. I'm well and truly in trouble now. They stop in an intimidating line, all three of them muscular and jacked up enough to knock a car over. Their black hair is all the same shade, likely because they are all cousins, I'm sure, and they have deeply tanned skin that doesn't match how pale my skin is. Considering I'm a foster kid, I could have at least gotten the same looks as them, but oh no, the moon goddess gave me bright blonde hair that never stops growing fast and freckly pale skin to stand out. I look like the moon comparing itself to the beauty of the sun with everyone in my pack.

Beta Valeriu takes a long sip of his drink, his eyes flashing green, his wolf making it clear he likes the hunt. Valeriu is the newest beta, taking over from his father, who recently retired at two hundred years of age and gave the role to his son willingly. But Valeriu is a dick. Simple as. He might be good-looking, like most of the five betas are, but each one of them lacks a certain amount of brain cells. The thing is, wolves don't need to be smart to be betas, they just need the right bloodline and to kill when the alpha clicks his fingers.

All wolves like to hunt and kill. And damn, I'm always the hunted in this pack.

"You know better than to run from us, little Mairin. Little Mary the lamb who runs from the wolf," he sing songs the last part, taking a slow step forward, his shoe grating across the dirt under his feet. Always the height jokes with this tool. He might be over six foot, and sure, my five foot three height isn't intimidating, but has no one heard the phrase *small but deadly?*

Even if I'm not even a little deadly. "Who invited you to my party?"

"The entire class in our pack was invited," I bite out.

He laughs, the crisp sound echoing around me like a wave of frost. "We both know you might be in this pack, but that's only because of the law about killing female children. Otherwise, our alpha would have ripped you apart a long time ago."

Yeah, I know the law. The law that states female children cannot be killed because of the lack of female wolves born into the pack. There is roughly one female to five wolves in the pack, and it's been that way for a long time for who knows what reason. So, when they found me in the forest at twelve, with no memories and nearly dead, they had to take me in and save my life.

A life, they have reminded me daily, has only been given to me because of that law. The law doesn't stop the alpha from treating me like crap under his shoe or beating me close to death for shits and giggles. Only me, though. The other foster kid I live with is male, so he doesn't get the "special" attention I do. Thankfully.

"We both know you can't kill me or beat me bad enough to attract attention without the alpha here. So why don't you just walk away and find some poor dumbass girl to keep you busy at the party?" I blurt out, tired of all this. Tired of never saying what I want to these idiots and fearing the alpha all the time. A bitter laugh escapes Valeriu's mouth as his eyes fully glow this time. So do his friends', as I realise I just crossed a line with my smart-ass mouth.

My foster carer always said my mouth would get me into trouble.

Seems he is right once again.

A threatening growl explodes from Beta Valeriu's chest, making all the hairs on my arms stand up as I take a step back just as he shifts. I've seen it a million times, but it's always amazing and terrifying at the same time. Shifter energy, pure dark forest green magic, explodes around his body as he changes shape. The only sound in the room is his clicking bones and my heavy, panicked breathing as I search for a way out of here once again, even though I know it's pointless.

I've just wound up a wolf. A beta wolf, one of the most powerful in our pack.

Great job, Irin. Way to stay alive.

The shifter magic disappears, leaving a big white wolf in the space where Valeriu was. The wolf towers over me, like most of them do, and its head is huge enough to eat me with one bite. Just as he steps forward to jump, and I brace myself for something painful, a shadow of a man jumps down from the broken slats above me, landing with a thump. Dressed in a white cloak over jeans and a shirt, my foster carer completely blocks me from Valeriu's view, and I sigh in relief.

"I suggest you leave before I teach you what an experienced, albeit retired, beta wolf can do to a young pup like yourself. Trust me, it will hurt, and our alpha will look the other way."

The threat hangs in the air, spoken with an authority that Valeriu could never dream of having in his voice at eighteen years old. The room goes silent, filled with thick tension for a long time before I hear the wolf running off, followed by two pairs of footsteps moving quickly. My badass foster carer slowly turns around, lowering his hood and brushing his long grey hair back from his face. Smothered in wrinkles, Mike is ancient, and to this day, I have no clue why he offered to work with the foster kids of the pack. His blue eyes remind me of the pale sea I saw once when I was twelve. He always dresses like a Jedi from the human movies, in long cloaks and swords clipped to his hips that look like lightsabres as they glow with magic, and he tells me this is his personal style.

His name is even more human than most of the pack names that get regularly overused. My name, which is the only thing I know about my past thanks to a note in my hand, is as uncommon as it gets. According to an old book on names, it means Their Rebellion, which makes no sense. Mike is apparently a normal human name, and from the little interaction I've had with humans through their technology, his name couldn't be more common.

"You are extremely lucky my back was playing up and I went for a walk, Irin," he sternly comments, and I sigh.

"I'm sorry," I reply, knowing there isn't much else I can say at this point. "The mating ceremony is tomorrow, and I wanted one night of being normal. I shouldn't have snuck out of the foster house."

"No, you should not have when your freedom is so close," he counters and reaches up, gently pinching my chin with his fingers and turning my head to the side. "Your lip is cut, and there is considerable bruising to your cheek. Do you like being beaten by those pups?"

"No, of course not," I say, tugging my face away, still tasting my blood in my mouth. "I wanted to be normal! Why is that so much to ask?"

"Normal is for humans and not shifters. It is why they gave us the United Kingdom and Ireland and then made walls around the islands to stop us from getting out. They want normal, and we need nothing more than what is here: our pack," he begins, telling me what I already know. They agreed three hundred years ago we would take this part of earth as our own, and the humans had the rest. No one wanted interbreeding, and this was the best way to keep peace. So the United Kingdom's lands were separated into four packs. One in England, one in Wales, one in Scotland and one in Ireland. Now there are just two packs, thanks to the shifter wars: the Ravensword Pack that is my home, who worship the moon goddess, and then the Fall Mountain Pack, who owns Ireland, a pack we are always at war with. Whoever they worship, it isn't our goddess, and everything I know about them suggests they are brutal. Unfeeling. Cruel.

Which is exactly why I've never tried to leave my pack to go there. It might be shit here, but at least it's kind of safe and I have a future. Of sorts.

"Do you think it will be better for me when I find my mate tomorrow?" I question...not that I want a mate who will control me with his shifter energy. But it means I will shift into a wolf, like every female can when they are mated, and I've always wanted that.

Plus, a tiny part of me wants to know who the moon goddess herself has chosen for me. The other half of my soul. My true mate. Someone who won't see me as the foster kid who has no family, and will just want me.

Mike looks down at me, and something unreadable crosses his eyes. He turns away and starts walking out of the abandoned house, and I jog to catch up with him. Snowflakes drop into my blonde hair as we head through the forest, back to the foster home, the place I will finally leave one way or another tomorrow. I pull my leather jacket around my chest, over my brown T-shirt for warmth. My torn and worn out jeans are soaked with snow after a few minutes of walking, the snow becoming thicker with every minute. Mike is silent as we walk past the rocks that mark the small pathway until we get to the top of the hill that overlooks the main pack city of Ravensword.

Towering buildings line the River Thames that flows through the middle of the city. The bright lights make it look like a reflection of the stars in the sky, and the sight is beautiful. It might be a messed up place, but I can't help but admire it. I remember the first time I saw the city from here, a few days after I was found and healed. I remember thinking I had woken up from hell to see heaven, but soon I learnt heaven was too nice of a word for this place. The night is silent up here, missing the usual noise of the people in the city, and I silently stare down wondering why we have stopped.

"What do you see when you look at the city, Irin?"

I blow out a long breath. "Somewhere I need to escape."

I don't see his disappointment, but I easily feel it.

"I see my home, a place with darkness in its corners but so much light. I see a place even a foster wolf with no family or ancestors to call on can find happiness tomorrow," he responds. "Stop looking at the stars for your escape, Irin, because tomorrow you will find your home in the city you are trying so hard to see nothing but darkness in."

He carries on walking, and I follow behind him, trying to do what he has asked, but within seconds my eyes drift up to the stars once again.

Because Mike is right, I am always looking for my way to escape, and I always will. I wasn't born in this pack, and I came from outside the walls that have been up for hundreds of years. That's the only explanation for how they found me in a forest with nothing more than a small glass bottle in my hand and a note with my name on it. No one knows how that is possible, least of all me, but somehow I'm going to figure it out. I have to.

CHAPTER

TWO

"Wake up. You have a book on your face."

Blinking my eyes open, I see nothing but blurry lines until I lift the book I was reading off my face and rub my nose. Damn, I must have fallen asleep reading again. I close the human-written romance book about demons at an academy and turn my gaze to where my foster brother is holding the door open. Jesper Perdita has dark brown, overgrown hair that falls around his face and shoulders, and his clothes are all a little too big for him and torn in places because they are hand-me-downs. But he smiles every single damn day, and for that alone, I love him. At just eight, he acts the same age as me thanks to losing his family a year ago and having no relatives offer to take him in. I don't care that we aren't blood-related, somehow I'm always going to be here for him, because he hasn't had a childhood any more than I have. We are foster kids in a pack that hates our very existence, and they make damn sure we know about it.

The fact they keep him alive is just because one day he might have a powerful wolf when he turns sixteen. If he doesn't, he won't have any family to save him from what happens next. I'm a little luckier in the sense I will find a mate, every female always does at the mating ceremony in the year they turn eighteen, and my mate will have no choice but to keep me alive. Even if he hates who I am, our fate is linked from the second the bond is shown.

"What time is it, Scrubs?" I ask, needing to pull my thoughts from the ceremony to anything else before I freak out. He twitches his nose at my nickname. That came from how many times he needed to scrub his face of dirt and mud every single day. He is the messiest kid I've ever seen, and it's awesome. I want a different future for him, one where he could have the same last name as everyone in the pack other than the foster kids. We are given the last name Perdita, which means *lost* in Latin, because we are lost in every sense of the word.

Everyone else in the pack shares the same last name as the pack alpha. Ravensword.

"Six in the morning. We have to leave for the

ceremony in an hour, and Mike said you need to bathe and wear the dress in the bathroom," he answers. He looks down, nervously kicking his foot. "Mike said something about brushing your hair so it doesn't look like a bat's nest."

I snort and run my hand through my blonde hair. Sure...I might not have brushed it a lot, but the unruly waves don't want to be tamed.

"I won't go, get a mate and never come back. You know that, right?" I ask him, sliding myself out of my warm bed and into the much colder room. Snowflakes line my bedroom window that is slightly cracked open, and I walk over, pushing it shut before looking back at Jesper. He meets my gaze with his bright blue eyes, but he says nothing.

"Whoever finds out you're their mate is going to want you to start fresh. Without this place and me following you around. I might be eight, but I'm not stupid," he replies. Floorboards creak under my feet as I walk over to him and pull him in for a hug, resting my head on top of his. The truth is, I can't promise him much. The males in mating have control over the females, and to resist that control is painful, so I'm told. That's why the moon goddess is the only one who can choose a mate for us, because if it went wrong, it would be a disaster for all involved.

"If my mate does, then I will figure out a way to get him to let me see you. The moon goddess will not give me a mate I am going to hate. All mates love each other," I tell him what I've heard.

"I don't like goodbyes," he replies, pulling away from me. "So I won't come with you today. I won't."

"I get it, kid," I say as he walks to the stairs. He never looks back, and I'm proud of him, even if it hurts to watch him make another choice that only adults should have to make. I head back into my small bedroom, which has a single bed with white sheets and a squeaky mattress, and one chest of drawers. I grab my towels and head down the stairs to the only bathroom in the old, very quirky house. The bathroom is through the first door in the corridor, and I shut the door behind me, not bothering to switch the light on as it is bright enough in here from the light pouring through the thin windows at the top of the room. Peeling dolphin-covered wallpaper lines every wall, and the porcelain clawfoot bathtub is right in the middle of the room. A cream toilet and a row of worn white cabinets line the other side, with a sink in the middle of them.

Hanging on the back of the door is the dress I have dreaded to see and yet wanted to because it's the nicest thing I am likely ever going to wear.

The mating dress is a custom-made dress for every woman in the pack, paid for by the alpha to celebrate the joy-filled day, and each is made to worship the moon goddess herself. Mine is no different. My dress is pure silk and softer than I could have imagined as I run my fingers over it. The hem of the dress is lined with sparkling white crystals, and the top part of the dress is tight around the chest and stomach. The bottom half falls like a ballgown, heavier than the top and filled with dozens of silk layers that shimmer as I move them.

As I stare at the dress, the urge to run away fills me. The urge to run to the sea and swim to the wall to see if there is any way to get out. Any way to escape the choices I have been given in life.

Mike was right, I can't see the light in the pack, because the darkness smothers too much. It takes too much.

I step away until the back of my legs hit the cold bathtub, and I sink down to the floor, wrapping my arms around my legs and resting my head on top of my knees.

One way or another, the mating ceremony is going to change everything for me.

"Do hurry, Irin. We have a four-hour drive, and this is not a day you should be late like every other day of your life!" Mike shouts through the door, banging on it twice.

"On it!" I shout back, crawling to my feet and pushing all thoughts of trying to escape to the back of my mind. It was a stupid idea, anyway. The pack lands are heavily guarded, and they would scent me a mile off. After a quick bath to wipe the dirt off me and wash my hair, I brush my wavy hair until it falls to my waist in bouncy locks, even when I know the wind will whip them up into a storm as soon as I'm outside. The dress is easy to slip on, and I wipe the mirror of the steam to look at myself after pulling my boots on.

My green eyes, the colour of moss mixed with specks of silver, look brighter this morning against my pale skin, framed by blonde, almost golden, hair. I look as terrified as I feel about today, but this is what the moon goddess wants, and she is our ancestor. The first wolf to howl at the moon and receive the power to shift.

She will not let me down today.

I nod at myself, like a total loser, and walk out

of the bathroom to find Mike and my other foster brother waiting for me. Mike huffs and walks away, mumbling something about a lamb to the slaughter under his breath, and I look at Daniel instead. His brown eyes are wide as he looks at me from head to toe, likely realising for the first time the best friend he has is actually a girl. He is used to me in jeans or baggy clothes, following him through the muddy forest and not giving a crap if every single one of my nails is broken by the end.

And I never wear dresses. Not like this. Daniel runs his hand through his muddy-brown hair that needs a cut before he smiles.

"Shit, you look different, Irin," he comments with a thick voice. Daniel is one year older than me, and when he was tested for his power last year, he was found to be an extremely powerful wolf. He is next in line to be a beta if anyone dies, which would be a big thing for a foster kid to be a beta. Either way, he is free of this place, and who knows, he might even be my mate. A small part of me hopes so because Daniel is my best friend, and it would be so easy to spend my life with him. I don't know about romance, as I have never seen him like that. He is good-looking in a rugged way, so I guess we could figure it out.

"Nervous about today?" I ask him, as this is his second mating ceremony, and it's likely he might find a mate. It's usually the second or third ceremony where males find their mates, but for females, it's always the first.

He clears his throat and meets my eyes. "Yeah, but who wouldn't be?"

"Me. I'm totally cool with it," I sarcastically reply. He laughs and walks over, pulling me into a tight hug like he always does. This time, I hear his wolf rumble in his chest, the vibrations shaking down my arms.

"If you're mated to a tool, I'll help you kill him and hide the body. Got it?" he tells me, and I laugh at his joke until he leans back, placing his hands on my shoulder. He moves one of his hands and tips my chin up so I'm looking at him. "I'm not joking, Irin. I don't care who it is, they aren't fucking around with you."

"Mates are always a perfect match," I reply, twitching my nose. "Why would you think—"

He lowers his voice as he cuts me off. "You don't live in the city like I do, and I can tell you now, mates are not a perfect match. Not even close. The moon goddess...well, I don't know what she is doing, but you need to be cautious. Very cautious because of your background."

"Why didn't you tell me this before?" I demand.

He shrugs. "Guess I didn't want you to over-think it and try to run. I can't save you from what they'd do if you ran, but I can protect you from a shitty mate. I.e., threaten to break every bone in his body if he hurts you."

"Daniel—" I'm cut off as Mike comes back into the corridor and clears his throat.

"Get in the car, now. It looks bad on me when we are late!" he huffs, holding the front door open. Daniel uses his charming smile to make Mike's lips twitch in laughter as I hurry to the front door and step out into the freezing cold snow. It sinks into my dress and shoes, but I welcome the icy stillness to the air, forcing me to stop over worrying for a second.

"Always daydreaming, this one," Mike mutters as he passes me, talking to Daniel at his side. "Her eyes are going to get stuck looking up in the clouds one day."

"At least I'd be seeing a pretty view for the rest of my life," I call after Mike as I hurry after them down the path to the old car waiting by the road. We don't use cars often, only today and travelling to funerals is permitted, mostly because the cars are old junk that make a lot of noise and take up fuel. Daniel pulls the yellow rusty door to the car open, and I slide inside to the opposite seat before doing up my seatbelt as Daniel and Mike get in the car. Mike drives and Daniel sits next to me rather than shotgun.

About ten minutes into the drive, I realise why Daniel sits next to me as my hands shake and he covers my hand with his.

Please, moon goddess, choose Daniel or someone decent. I don't want to become a mate murderer in my first year as a wolf.

CHAPTER

THREE

Flickering, multicoloured lights drift across my eyes as I wake up, finding my head lying on Daniel's broad shoulder, his arm wrapped around my waist, and it's so unexpected, I jolt up, almost hitting my head against Daniel's chin. He moves super fast, with reflexes his wolf gives him, and just misses my head. I slide out of Daniel's arm, and he clears his throat, straightening up on his seat and running a hand through his thick hair. Rather than talk about that awkward moment, I turn and look out the window, frost stuck to its edges, to see we are driving down by a cliff that overlooks the glittering sea between Wales and Ireland. I've been to this place once when I was fifteen on a school trip to see where a mating ceremony is held and what we should expect for our future.

If anywhere in this world made me believe in magic, it was this place. A place that has been in my dreams for so many years. For most wolves, this is the place they will meet their wolves and start their new life. For me, it's a way of escaping my past and finally finding out what the moon goddess wants for me. It can't be this life I have, the torture at the hands of pack leaders, the pain of being an outcast with no family.

I catch Mike's eyes in the middle mirror and see a little sadness in them like always, because he has heard and seen all the horrors the pack has forced on me throughout the years. Protecting me was something he has struggled to do, because, at the end of the day, he couldn't be everywhere.

"Nearly here, aren't we?" Daniel interrupts my thoughts, and I'm thankful for it. That's a dark memory lane to go down. "They should let you wear a coat over the dress, it's freezing."

"I've never cared about the cold," I remind him, gazing back out of the window as we pull up in the gravelled area by the cliff. Several groups of people are standing around or walking down the stone cliff pathway to the beach that is marked with fire lanterns on wooden poles every few metres, making the walk look eerie and frightening.

"You can do this, Irin. You've been brave ever since you were found in the woods, half-starved, dirty and alone. Look at you now," Mike tells me as he turns the car off, meeting my line of sight through the mirror. "You are a woman this pack will be honoured to have. Now hold your head high, put the past away and show them. Show them who you are, Irin."

My cheeks feel red and hot as I wipe a few tears away and force my hands to stop shaking as I grab the handle of the door. I can't tell him, not without my voice catching, that I will miss Mike and his words of wisdom. His kindness and general attitude towards life, the ways he has shown me how to be strong even at my lowest points. Pulling the door handle open, I step out onto the lightly snow-covered ground, and the cold, brittle sea air slams into me, making me shiver from head to toe. I can taste the salt in the air and smell the water of the sea and hear it crashing against the sand below us. The wind whips my hair around my face as Daniel walks past me, looking back once before he walks down the path to join the other men at the beach where they have to stand. Mike moves to my side, and we simply wait as all the men leave for the path down to the beach, while the women, us, wait at the top for our time to descend.

Some parents linger for a while before they walk

to the edge of the cliff in the distance where there's a massive crowd of spectators waiting to watch the magic of the mating ceremony. Mike leaves eventually to join them, never glancing back at me. The girls all gather, pretending I don't exist like they always have done since I turned up at their school. A small, tiny part of me hurts that not a single one of the forty-two girls in my class who have known me six years even looks my way.

I'm invisible to them, to my pack, to everyone.

Rubbing my chest, I gulp when the bell rings. A single, beautiful bell ring fills the air to start the beginning of the mating ceremony, and tension rings through the air as everyone goes silent. Like ducks in a row, the women all line up, and of course I move right to the back, behind Lacey Ravensword, someone who has never even looked my way, even though she is considered a low potential mate because of her father trying to run away from the pack, and he was killed when she was a toddler. Even she, with her family basically betrayers to the alpha himself, is higher ranked than I am. She flicks her dark brown hair over her shoulder, glancing back at me and sneering once with her beautiful face before turning away.

The cold seeps into my bones by the time the

line moves enough for me to walk, and my legs feel stiff with every step, the nerves making me feel so close to passing out right here and now. Every single step off the cliff and down the path feels torturous until I see the beach.

Then everything fades into nothing but pure magic. In the centre of the sandy yellow beach is a massive archway, sculpted into two wolves with their noses touching where they meet in the middle. The wolves are so high the tips of their ears touch the heavy clouds above us, and icicles line the grooves of the fur on their snow-tipped backs. In the centre of the archway, one of the first females steps into the pool of water under the archway, sinking all the way under completely before rising and swimming slowly through the archway. The water suddenly glows green, lit up with magic from the moon goddess herself.

The young lady with long black hair climbs out of the pool on the other side, her entire body glowing green with magic, and the magic slowly slips from her skin, turning itself into a swirling ball of energy and shooting away from her. It flies into the crowd of wolf shifter men waiting on the other side, all of them too hard to really see from here, and there are cheers when the mate or mates are no doubt found. I can't see who the female goes to as the cliff winds around, but I hope she is happy with her new mates. Daniel's warnings about mates not always being happy fills my mind, making me more nervous than ever before, because what if he is right? What if I end up with a mate who I hate and he hates me?

I trip on a small rock, slamming down onto the path and hissing as my hand is cut. I look up as Lacey turns back, and then she just laughs, leaving me on my knees on the path as she carries on behind the queue. Tears fill my eyes that I refuse to let fall, and I stand up, seeing my dress is now dirty with sand and mud, and I lift my hand to see blood dripping down my palm to my wrist from a long cut. Sighing, I close my palm and let my blood drop against the wet sand as I know I have to carry on down this path.

What feels like forever later, I get to the beach and look across to see Lacey waiting behind three other classmates, just as one of them steps into the water. Four left before my fate is decided. I'm tempted to slip my shoes off, to enjoy the feel of the cold sand under my bare feet, but I keep my boots on. I don't want to lose them. I walk over the beach, feeling so many eyes watching and judging me. I refuse to look at the men on the other side, knowing the new alpha will be there, and seeing him brings up so many dark memories. He was just the alpha's son back then, back when we were fifteen and he tricked me by pretending to be my friend.

Now he is the alpha, at only eighteen, after he ripped his father to pieces four months ago. The pack is scared of him, but me?

He terrifies me.

Keeping my eyes down, I only look up to see Lacey step into the water with perfect poise and elegance I could never master in my wildest dreams. She sinks under the water, and it glows bright green, and this close, I can feel the magic like it's pulling me towards it. The water is enchanting, and I can't take my eyes off it until the glow fades, and I glance up to see the magic surrounding Lacey as she stands on the other side of the pool. The magic leaves her body and gathers in a ball, before slamming left and straight into the chest of one of the men near the front.

Not just any man.

Daniel.

He stands in pure shock, looking at the green magic bouncing around his skin before he looks up at Lacey, and then he turns to me. Our eyes meet, and silently I try to tell him it's okay.

Even when it feels like a storm has just started in my chest and that storm is going to take every bit of hope from me.

Daniel doesn't move for a long time, and Lacey follows his gaze back to me, her eyes narrowing as I quickly look away and back to the water. Out of the corner of my eye, I see Lacey walk to Daniel, and he places his hand on her back, leading her away from the crowd and towards the pathway to the crowds of people waiting at the top of the cliff to celebrate with them. To cheer about their mating.

And now it's my turn.

Everything is silent, even the violent sea and snow-filled sky seem to still for this moment as I take a step forward and my foot sinks into the warm water. It instantly glows green, so bright it hurts my eyes, and pulls me in, my body almost betraying my fear-filled mind as I sink into the water until my head falls under. The green light becomes blinding as I float in the water, seeing nothing but light, until a voice fills my mind.

"You are my chosen, Irin. My chosen."

Something appears in my hand as I'm pushed up to the surface, and I gasp as I rise out of the water on the other side, almost stumbling to my feet on the sand, seeing the green magic swirling around my body in thick waves. It bounces, almost violently, in swirls and waves before pulling away from me into a giant ball of green magic, much bigger than anyone else's.

Why the hell do I have to stand out in this of all things? With so many people watching? I can't bear to look or hear anyone as I watch the sphere of magic spin in the air before shooting across the sand right into the man in the middle of the pack.

A man of my nightmares.

A man who took my innocence, crushed it, and made me fear him.

The alpha of my pack.

*T*he silence is damning. Damning and hollow as I stare into the unfeeling hazel eyes of the wolf shifter who is apparently my fated mate. An alpha doesn't share his mate, so this is the only man in the entire world who the moon goddess believes I should be with. And he is a monster. The alpha doesn't move as green magic crackles around his body, picking up his fur cloak that hangs off his large shoulders. Thick black hair falls to his shoulders in a straight line, not a strand out of place, and his stern face is stoic as he looks at me. Water drips down my dress, my wet hair sticking to my shoulders, and all the warmth from the water is gone now. The magic is gone, replaced only with fear for what happens next.

"No."

His single word rings out across the beach to me, the few yards that are between us are like nothing. No. No to the mating? No, it being me the moon goddess chose as the alpha's mate?

I agree with him...hell no. Mating with this excuse of an alpha, a man with no soul and a scar on his chin I caused when I was fifteen, is a life I would rather not live. Only once have I ever thought about giving up on my life, once on a wintry day like this, caused by the same man I'm looking at right now. This is the second time I have wanted to give up completely.

Whispers and gasps from the crowd of wolves behind him and from the crowds on the cliff finally reach my ears, and I try to block out what they are saying even when some of their words are perfectly heard.

"Her? The alpha's mate? Disgusting!"

"Maybe the moon goddess made a terrible mistake."

"He should kill her and be done with it."

The whispers never stop, and the same thing is chanted as the alpha's eyes bleed from hazel to green, his wolf taking over. Then he takes one step forward towards me, and I itch to run, to turn and leave as fast as I can, but something tells me not to.

Maybe that bit of stubborn pride I have left. Mike always said pride is a bigger killer than any man. I can see his point as my legs refuse to move and I stay still as a deer caught in a wolf's gaze. The alpha walks right up to me, his closeness making me feel sick to my stomach as he grabs my throat and lifts me slightly off the ground. Not enough to strangle me or cut my airways off, but enough to make me gasp, to make me want to struggle. I claw at his arm to get him off, but I'm nothing but a fly buzzing around a cake to him. I can see it in his eyes, his eyes owned by his wolf.

"How did you trick the moon goddess herself into believing a rat like you could ever be an alpha's mate?" he demands, and when I don't answer, he shakes me harshly, tightening his grip for a second. A second enough for me to scream and gasp, coughing on air when he loosens his grip. He shakes his head, his eyes bleeding from green back to hazel. To think I once trusted those hazel eyes, I dreamt about them, I thought he was my real friend.

"I asked you a question, Irin."

"My name is Mairin to you, not Irin. M-my friends call me Irin, Alpha Sylvester Ravensword. Kill me if you're going to do it. I have feared you for so long that you killing me is nothing more than the goddess giving me my wish."

The lie falls from my tongue easily, even if his name does not. The moon goddess never gave me my real wish, my wish I begged her for once, to kill him, the alpha's son, Sylvester Ravensword. Instead, in some twisted version of fate, she made him alpha and me his mate he has waited for. His eyes stay hazel, but in the corners I see the green struggling to take over. He slowly tightens his grip around my neck, and I close my eyes, wanting to see nothing in these last moments. I gasp as I struggle to breathe, instinctively smacking and scratching at his one hand holding me up by the neck. Fear and panic take over, making my eyes pop open just as I'm thrown across the sand. With a slam, I hit the hard sand on my side, and a cracking noise in my arm is followed by incredible pain as I scream.

"Irin!" I hear Daniel shout in the distance, a wolfy and deep noise just before a foot slams into my stomach once. Then twice, then again and again. The pain almost becomes numb when my voice gives out, and the kicks finally stop as I roll onto my back, looking up at Alpha Sylvester as he angrily kicks me one more time before stepping back, rubbing his hands over his face repeatedly.

"No one follows us. If anyone does, I will rip them to shreds," I hear Alpha Sylvester demand,

and the noise of wolves fighting nearby mixes with the sound of the waves. A hand digs into my hair and pulls me up as I taste blood in my mouth. Everything is blurry as someone drags me by my hair and arm over sharp rocks that cut into my back and catch on my dress, but part of me detaches from my body, drifting into a world of no pain as I fade in and out of consciousness. Eventually I'm dropped onto grass, and I blink my eyes a few times, coughing on the blood in my mouth and turning my head to the side, every inch of my body hurting so badly the pain threatens to knock me out with every breath. A hand wraps around my throat once more, and I'm lifted into the air, my feet hanging as I struggle to breathe.

"Open your eyes," Alpha Sylvester demands, his fiery breath blowing across my face.

Opening my eyes is harder than I thought it would be, and when I do, I see he is right in front of me.

"I can't kill you, because my wolf will not allow it." He shakes me once. "Die in the sea for your fated mate, Irin. Die like you should have so many years ago, because if the sea does not take you, I will know. I will know, and I will never stop sending wolves to kill you. I have rejected you as my mate, you are not worthy of me, and you never could be. You are nothing."

"Then why does the moon goddess think other-wise?" I whisper back with all the strength I have. I should plead for my life, I should beg and cry, but I just stare at him as his eyes flash with pure anger, and he roars as he lets me go. The wind cannot catch my body as I fly off the cliff, well aware the sea is going to take my life in seconds.

And in those seconds I fall, I still pray to the moon goddess for someone to catch me.

CHAPTER

FIVE

"Get the healer ready!" a deep voice demands, nothing more than a groggy sound to my sore ears as I struggle to wake up. Coldness like I've never known controls my body from head to toe, and it's not just cold, I'm soaking wet too. Every inch of my body hurts. Even my eyelids ache as I pull them open to see rocks in front of me. Smooth white rocks. Waves crash in the distance, and I can smell nothing but damp water. Lifting my head, which takes more strength than I thought it would, I see I'm still in my mating ceremony dress, but it's ripped around my stomach, and a large cut snakes down my ribs, hidden under the ripped fabric of my dress. My bare feet are stuck in the wet sand, and I'm curled up in a space between a group of rocks like the sea threw me here.

Flashes of memories attack me quickly. The sea. The mating ceremony. The alpha who was meant to be my mate but instead tried to kill me... How am I alive?

Scuffling of heavy booted feet reminds me I'm not alone, and I jump away from the noise behind me, pivoting to see a man standing on the rock. His silhouette blocks out the light, making all around him glow as I drift my eyes up his body. Thick black trousers cover large thighs, and he has a black shirt tucked into them. The shirt stretches across his large shoulders, large enough to make him a champ at a rugby match if he chose it. Following my eyes up over his golden skin, I suck in a deep breath when I see his face.

He is beautiful in a way men shouldn't be allowed to be. Strong jawline, high cheekbones, perfectly shaped lips and thick black eyelashes that surround clear blue eyes that remind me of a lake— still, in an eerie way that makes you wonder if there is any life below the waters. Black locks of hair that are a little too long, falling just over his eyes when the wind blows, look softer than the silk dress I'm wearing.

No one in my pack ever looked like him. I would have noticed.

The more I stare, the longer I realise he is staring right back at me, like he has seen a ghost.

Like I'm familiar to him. Considering where I came from, he might have done. Not that I have a clue where we are. I lean up on my one arm, but I can't see out of the rocks or anything around the man standing over me.

Correction: the wolf. He is watching me like a wolf, that I am certain of. He is too direct, too inhuman like, and all that I need to see now is his eyes glow.

"Do you know me?" I ask, my voice throaty, and I clear it, tasting nothing but thick salt left over from the sea.

The man tilts his head to the side. "Why are you here?"

"I-I was..." I pause because I have no idea where I am, and telling this wolf I'm the alpha's rejected mate might not be the best idea if I'm still in Ravensword lands. He will drag me back to the alpha, who will try to kill me again. No, I can't do that.

"Answer me."

The man's command is clear, ringing with power and frustration. I look up, meeting his eyes once more even when I can't think straight or of a single word to say. Whatever I say is going to get me killed, and I can't help but think I've been given a second chance at life. I should never have survived falling into the sea, not with the injuries I have, not when I passed out, but here I am. Alive.

It's clear the moon goddess has much more planned for me than I know.

When I don't say a word for a long time, he moves. The man moves so quickly, and within seconds he is in my face, leaning over me on the rocks. His nose gently touches mine, my body a mix with fear and curiosity.

"Tell me," he commands once more. "Tell me why you are on the shores of the Fall Mountain Pack, or you will die this very second."

Fall Mountain Pack?

Oh my god... How am I alive and on this island? I know people usually die who try to swim between the islands, but for me to have gotten here unconscious is nothing short of magic. I'm yet to decide what kind of magic, considering all I know about the Fall Mountain Pack is that they are cruel and vicious. That they live in ways most wolves would never do or even think about. They don't trade with the Ravensword Pack, and every attempt at peace has been met with death. We are told they are monsters, and now I'm on their lands.

But truthfully, I'm dead either way. If they send

me back, the alpha will kill me, and if I stay here, it's likely they will kill me.

I have nothing to lose by telling this man the truth.

"My name is Mairin Perdita, and I am a rejected mate of the Ravensword Pack," I announce, leaning back against the rocks and curling my legs underneath myself, needing space from his man. His eyes widen, but he doesn't say a word. "The mating ceremony named me as the alpha's mate, and because I am a foster child with no family or worth, he rejected me. After hurting me in anger, he tried to kill me by throwing me off a cliff. How I'm here, alive, is a mystery to me, but I guess I am asking for your help. I'm asking for a damn miracle, because my life has been anything but one."

"I would wager surviving your rejection is a miracle. The sea is a cruel mistress at the best of times, and last night was one of the worst storms seen in years," he finally replies, leaning back, his voice less hostile than it was. "I can always tell when someone is lying to me, and you are not, Mairin Perdita. My name is Alpha Henderson Fall, and I am going to help you."

"You're the alpha?" I whisper in shock and a

little fear. It shouldn't surprise me he is so high in rank, just because of how commanding and powerful he comes across as, but it does.

"One of the four," he answers and moves closer. "You are weak, my wolf senses it, and I must carry you. Will you allow me? It is a twenty-minute walk to the lighthouse where there is a healer."

The part of me that hates being touched, especially by men, makes me want to say no and stubbornly try to climb out of these rocks myself. But I know I can't. Every inch of me hurts, my stomach is bleeding, and my ankle looks swollen. Somehow I have survived the sea, but without help, I will not survive much longer. I nod once, unable to actually agree, and I'm sure my hesitancy shines in my eyes as he comes closer and wraps his arms underneath me before effortlessly picking me up. In order to steady myself, my hands go out around his neck, brushing against a necklace there that is tucked into his shirt. Henderson jumps out of the rocks, and I look around me to see a tall mountain right in front of us, and a small forest lies between the beach and the mountain. The mountain is topped with snow, and several caves look like they have lights inside from this distance. The beach is long with rocky sand and harsh waves that crash against everything they hit, and in the distance, I see a faded blue light-house with its bright light turning in circles. Henderson is silent as he jumps off the rocks into the sand and eats up the space between us and the lighthouse with his enormous steps. After a few minutes, I relax my shoulders a little.

"Is it just luck you found me, or do you live around here?" I question.

Henderson looks down at me, his blue eyes hard to read. "What do you know of my pack, Mairin?"

"That you are monsters," I tell him, remembering well how he said he could sense if I was lying.

His lips tilt up into a dazzling smile. "Lies are so easily told to those who live in fear, and your alpha lied, Mairin. We were never the monsters, but our life differs greatly from where you have come from. Here we don't have fated mates, we only mate with who we fall in love with. Wolves are free to date, to explore, to do whatever they want, and the only new wolves we accept into the pack are rejected or lost. We respect loyalty, and we take in those who are nothing to others."

"There have been other rejected mates?" I ask.

His smile falls. "I collect over one wolf a week from this shore. All of them rejected and thrown into the sea because their mate could not convince their wolf to kill them."

"I had no idea," I whisper.

"To answer your question," Henderson states, shifting me a little in his arms, "I do not live here, but I am called to the lighthouse every day to check out who has arrived. If you had lied to me, or if you were someone who just escaped the pack, then I am tasked with ending your life. We do not take in those who desert their pack and family. We want only those who will be loyal."

My heart beats fast in my chest, hearing the sincerity of his voice. He would have killed me. "So you kill for loyalty?"

"No, I kill for my pack," he answers, his tone clarifying that is the last of our conversation, and I rest back, watching the sea and the very outline of the land in the distance, hidden by clouds. All I can think of is Daniel and Jesper, and even Mike. I have to hope they look after each other, because I can't ever go back.

The Ravensword alpha is my mate, and he will do worse than reject me next time, he will have someone kill me.

So I have to make the Fall Mountain Pack my new home, whatever it takes.

Made in the USA
Columbia, SC
18 July 2024

38812842R00181